'I don't unde[rstand.]'

Erika looked at hi[m.]

'No, I don't eith[er,' Noah agreed with a] similar kind of bewilderment. 'I can't believe the amount of personal time and energy you appear to have expended on some of my elderly patients.'

Erika's eyes blazed. 'I would've thought I was just doing my job.'

'Bunkum! Your sense of dedication terrifies me. And why risk burning yourself out for the sake of a list of patients you're not likely to see again? Why, Erika?'

Leah Martyn's writing career began at age eleven, when she wrote the winning essay in the schoolwork section of a country show. As an adult, success with short stories led her to try her hand at a longer work. With her daughter training to become a Registered Nurse, the highs and lows of hospital life touched a chord, and writing Medical Romances™ liberally spiked with humour became a reality. Home is with her husband in semi-rural Queensland. Her hobbies include an involvement with live theatre and relaxing on the beach with a good book.

Recent titles by the same author:

ALWAYS MY VALENTINE

FOR PERSONAL REASONS

BY
LEAH MARTYN

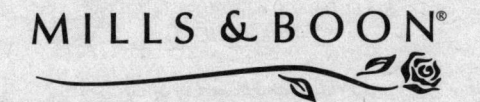

MILLS & BOON

> **DID YOU PURCHASE THIS BOOK WITHOUT A COVER?**
>
> If you did, you should be aware it is **stolen property** as it was reported *unsold and destroyed* by a retailer. Neither the author nor the publisher has received any payment for this book.

All the characters in this book have no existence outside the imagination of the author, and have no relation whatsoever to anyone bearing the same name or names. They are not even distantly inspired by any individual known or unknown to the author, and all the incidents are pure invention.

All Rights Reserved including the right of reproduction in whole or in part in any form. This edition is published by arrangement with Harlequin Enterprises II B.V. The text of this publication or any part thereof may not be reproduced or transmitted in any form or by any means, electronic or mechanical, including photocopying, recording, storage in an information retrieval system, or otherwise, without the written permission of the publisher.

This book is sold subject to the condition that it shall not, by way of trade or otherwise, be lent, resold, hired out or otherwise circulated without the prior consent of the publisher in any form of binding or cover other than that in which it is published and without a similar condition including this condition being imposed on the subsequent purchaser.

MILLS & BOON and MILLS & BOON with the Rose Device are registered trademarks of the publisher.

*First published in Great Britain 2000
Harlequin Mills & Boon Limited,
Eton House, 18-24 Paradise Road, Richmond, Surrey TW9 1SR*

© Leah Martyn 2000

ISBN 0 263 82243 5

*Set in Times Roman 10½ on 12½ pt.
03-0006-39541*

*Printed and bound in Spain
by Litografía Rosés, S.A., Barcelona*

CHAPTER ONE

NOAH needed a locum.

But so far there'd been only a tepid response to his advertisements. Doctors, it seemed, didn't want to work in the bush these days. At least those worth employing, he thought drily.

Impatiently, he pushed a hand through his thick dark hair. He'd be a sure bet for the funny farm if he didn't get a holiday soon. Two years without a decent break was not being fair to his patients, and certainly wasn't doing his concentration any favours either...

'Fax just came for you.' Jenny McGill, the practice secretary-cum-everything popped her head around his door. 'Could be your answer.'

'Not a locum?'

'Could be.' Jenny smiled coyly, handing him the printout. 'It's from a girl.'

'A girl!' Noah's voice flew up several octaves.

Jenny clicked her tongue. 'Stop posturing and read it. She may be well qualified and employable.'

Noah gave a muttered response. 'Can't imagine a young female on a night-call up in the wild country around the Eldridge property, can you?'

'That's sexist, Noah. Women have been known to pitch in and do amazing things when they have to. And whatever—' she aimed a warning finger at her boss '—don't you dare take off and leave us to the mercy of old Archie Vidler!'

Noah managed a weary chuckle. 'He's offered, you know. Told me even though he's almost eighty he's as fit as a flea and still reads all his medical journals.'

Jenny flapped a dismissive hand. 'I'll bring you a coffee before afternoon surgery.'

'Erika Somers.' Noah murmured the name at the head of the faxed information. Then, pulling his chair closer to the desk, he prepared to read Dr Somers' letter and attached CV.

Impressive, he thought a few minutes later, scraping his fingers thoughtfully back and forth across his jaw. She'd acquired her medical degree in Melbourne. Post-grad at the city's Prince Alfred. Well, that was a baptism of fire for a start. Subsequently she'd worked as an SHO at the Royal Free in London, and more recently completed her GP training including a rural component.

With those kinds of credentials she could have worked anywhere. Noah's lips pursed in conjecture. So why, Erika Somers, would you choose to be a locum? More particularly, a locum in this rather isolated little border town in southern Queensland?

Noah's clear blue eyes were full of speculation as he tipped back his head and stared at the ceiling.

* * *

Erika needed answers.

Working as Noah Jameson's locum had its drawbacks, she decided ruefully, opening the door of her silver Laser and climbing in. And today, for some reason, she was feeling the isolation of being the only doctor for miles.

Hillcrest might be a gem as far as country towns went, with air as crisp as the apples grown in the orchards that ran right up into the hills. But right at this moment she'd have given anything to have been back in Melbourne with access to her medical network.

Swinging her car out on to the main road, she put her foot down, her frustration evident. There had to be something about her young patient's condition she was missing—or misinterpreting.

For a second she considered phoning her father in Melbourne and tapping into his medical knowledge, but just as quickly rejected the idea. He hadn't been exactly enthusiastic about her taking the locum's job anyway, declaring it to be the wrong career move for her.

Thinking of her father made her reflect on her other life in Melbourne, and Alistair waiting for her answer. In her mind's eye his fair hair and ready smile dipped in front of her vision. He wanted to marry her.

And he'd been so understanding about her wanting this time away to sort out her feelings. But ruefully she admitted she was no nearer a decision.

'Sorry, Alistair.' She gave a jagged little sigh, pulling into the car park adjoining the surgery.

Mid-afternoon sun bounced firelight off her fall of straight auburn hair as she crossed the strip of lawn to the practice. Mounting the front stairs, she looked around her, the action renewing her pleasure in Noah's set-up.

Jenny had told her he'd purchased the old Queenslander two years ago and had it refurbished as a medical facility. It was ideal, Erika thought, almost enviously, with its high-ceilinged rooms and wraparound verandahs. There was space and lots of it.

Pausing on the verandah, she looked out at the heat-hazed landscape, feeling her stomach clench. It had all happened so insidiously, but slowly, surely, she was being drawn into the life of this place. She was going to hate to have to leave when the time came…

And all this mooning isn't solving Joey's problem, she thought practically, turning to slide the key into the lock. Something caught her attention and she hesitated and drew back. Noah's surgery door was open by the tiniest margin, showing a chink of light. Her throat dried. She was positive she'd locked the door after her morning surgery…

Her heart leapt, banging a drumbeat against her ribs. Panic almost closed her throat. Could someone be searching for drugs? Dear God—

She clamped her teeth on her bottom lip, head to one side, listening. But there was no sound of anyone searching for anything. Perhaps they'd been and gone.

Taking a deep breath, she pulled herself together, and almost in slow motion began to push the door open...

'Oh—it's you!' Erika blinked her shock. 'W-what are you doing here? I wasn't expecting you for another week.'

Noah spun round from the window, his dark brows snapping together. Good grief! She looked ready to faint dead away. 'Sit down!' he ordered sharply, grabbing one of the patients' chairs and sliding it under her.

Erika felt her limbs suddenly boneless. Slumping into the chair, she clattered her keys on to the desktop. 'I thought you were a burglar—'

Noah scoffed a laugh. 'Do I look like a burglar?' Filling a glass from the water cooler, he placed it in front of her. 'And if I had been, Dr Somers, what were you intending to do? Stun me with your bag and wrestle me to the floor?'

She should be so lucky! Erika blocked a hoot of dry laughter. Noah Jameson was all male. Impressive height, broad shoulders and not bad-looking either. Her eyelashes fluttered down and then up again, absorbing his strong features as he sat in profile next to her on the edge of the desk. She took a mouthful of water.

'You shouldn't have been skulking in here in the first place.'

'Skulking!' He made a sound halfway between a snort and a laugh.

'You look better for your break away,' she sidetracked coolly, tilting her head to look at him.

'I feel remarkably fit.' His grin was slow, dizzyingly sexy. 'Amazing what a few early nights can achieve.'

Erika's unblinking regard suggested it wasn't merely early nights that had put the spring back in his step. In fact she could hardly believe the change in him.

On the two days she'd spent with him before he'd gone on leave he'd seemed off-hand, jaded, and she'd suspected somewhat ruefully he wouldn't have noticed if she'd been bald and sporting a couple of black eyes.

She guessed, with the oddest little twist of awareness, she was now looking at the real Noah Jameson, relaxed, clear-eyed, his whole manner upbeat.

She sent him a contained little smile. 'Why *are* you back early anyway? Checking up on me?'

'Should I be?'

She shrugged. 'I haven't managed to kill off any of your patients so far.'

'Not fishing for compliments, are you, Doctor?' His eyes fixed her with a brilliant blueness, before he slid off the edge of the desk and resumed his seat. 'By the way, I've looked over your daysheets. You've been busy.'

'Surely you're not surprised?' With a small defensive action, she lifted a hand and flicked a strand of hair behind her ear. 'Besides, I felt obliged to earn my keep.'

Noah didn't doubt she had. Not for a minute. His eyes narrowed thoughtfully. 'Have you managed any time off in the month you've been here?'

'Don't worry about me, Dr Jameson,' she said lightly. 'I'm fine.' The concern in his eyes, in his voice, had disconcerted her, in some way personalising what was after all a straight-out business arrangement. She swallowed uncomfortably. 'Are you intending to take your last week of leave or should I start packing?'

'Yes and no, in that order. I'm really only back this weekend to have my vehicle serviced and collect a few clothes.' He squinted at his watch. 'The Land Rover should be ready in another hour or so, and then I'll be out of your hair.'

So soon? Erika felt her spirits drop like a stone. Despite his sudden appearance, the fright he'd given her, she realised with a little shock she'd been ridiculously pleased to see him. Hiding her confusion, she hurriedly lifted her glass and took another mouthful of water.

Noah hadn't missed a beat of her guarded scrutiny, and again he wondered why she'd chosen to bury herself in such an outflung community and under such a mountain of work. She couldn't have money worries. He'd done enough checking to know she was from an old-established professional family in Melbourne.

His mouth firmed. And why should he care about her personal life anyway? She'd be gone in a matter of days. And he'd be back in charge of his practice again. Almost roughly, he shovelled a hand through his hair, wondering why the thought didn't seem to fill him with the pleasure it should.

'Noah...' Erika directed a slightly hesitant look at him. 'If you're not pressed for time, could I trouble you for a second opinion?'

'Fire away.' Folding his arms, he looked at her, his eyes razor-sharp with interest.

'Do you know the Bodetti family?' she asked.

Noah shook his head. 'The name doesn't ring any bells. Who's the patient?'

'The sixteen-year-old son, Joey. I admitted him to hospital this morning.' She made a small face. 'The communication with the parents isn't great. They have limited English and my Italian is abysmal. I've no idea whether I got through to them.'

'What's the problem with Joey?'

Erika shrugged. 'That's just it. I'm getting mixed signals but I'm reasonably sure we're looking at the onset of rheumatoid arthritis.'

'Bit young for that, isn't he?' Noah looked doubtful. 'Fill me in.'

'His parents brought Joey into the surgery about three weeks ago. He'd been off-colour, couldn't get out of bed, pain in his joints. He said his head was splitting.'

'And?' Noah's heavy-lidded eyes widened.

'I thought it was flu-related and prescribed accordingly.'

'And that worked?'

'Well—it seemed to. Joey returned to school, but out of the blue this morning he collapsed, playing soccer for his team. Obviously he needs further tests. I should be making arrangements to have him transferred to Brisbane. But the parents...' She palmed her hands expressively.

'Proving an obstacle, are they?' Noah gave a grunt of dry humour, having been there and been part of a similar scenario.

'Watching everything I do like hawks. And it's understandable,' she allowed quickly. 'But I just feel hamstrung with the lack of real communication. I mean, it's a hell of a thing to think I may have to tell them their son could have permanent functional disability to look forward to.'

'On the other hand,' Noah said calmly, 'you may be jumping the gun. Have you taken blood?'

'Of course. But there's no flight out until Monday.'

He got to his feet, turning abruptly to gather up her day-sheets he'd been reading and easing them back into the steel filing cabinet. Closing the drawer precisely, he locked it. 'Let's take a look at him, shall we?'

'You've a terrific set-up here,' Erika said as they made their way to the front of the building. Already the airy, pastel-coloured rooms had become a home away from home for her.

Noah grinned. 'Took a bit of convincing the bank, but it appears to have paid off. At least we're not all tripping over one another like we were in the original place. Are you getting on all right with Jen?' Courteously, he held the door open for his locum.

Erika's mouth tipped. 'Absolutely. She's shoved me back on the right track from time to time when I was floundering.'

'Good.' He looked pleased. 'Jenny knows the town and its inhabitants inside out. It helps.'

'The car's not locked,' she said when they got to the Laser. She shot him a wry look before she slipped on her sunglasses. 'Sorry about the space— or lack of it. Do you want to move the seat back?'

'Mmm.' Noah looked a bit dubious. 'Perhaps I'd better. Don't want to get cut off at the knees.'

They settled in and belted up. Chewing her lip, Erika wondered why her heart was beating like a small fist inside her chest. Was it Noah Jameson's proximity? Surely not. He was merely a colleague, if not technically her boss.

'Jenny said you have some Italian.' She swung her head around, sending little strands of hair swishing against his shoulder.

Noah adjusted his seatbelt. 'I did a crash course with the Dante Society when I began to negotiate to buy the practice. There's a high percentage of Italian migrants or their offspring in the district.'

'I had noticed.' Erika's comment was touched

with dry humour. Still smiling, she flicked on the switch and ignited the engine.

The Hillcrest community hospital was situated on the other side of the town, a cement block structure perched high to capture the view of distant mountains. Its ten-bed facility serviced the needs of the local residents and those of the outlying farming population.

'Here we are.' Erika reined in her faint trepidation with a taut smile and pulled into the parking space she'd vacated such a short time ago. 'Noah...' She turned to him hesitantly, her arm resting on the steering wheel. 'Mr and Mrs Bodetti will be with Joey. I couldn't prise them away. They're in their fifties, over-protective—'

'Say no more.' His eyes narrowed. 'I'll tread gently. I suppose it's too much to hope Anne Bryson is the RN in charge this shift?'

Erika smiled. 'Hopes fulfilled. She is.'

The charge nurse was just coming out of her office as they approached the nurses' station. 'Well, hello, you two.' Anne's small dark head tilted pertly. 'Couldn't live without the sight of us, I see, Noah?'

He grinned. 'Something like that. How're things, Annie?'

'Busy but bearable.' She smiled.

Erika chimed in hastily. 'Noah has offered to have a look at the Bodetti boy, Anne. I guess the parents are still with him?'

'Afraid so.' The RN shot her an apologetic half-smile. 'I did try to coax them to take a break, but no luck. The poor kid must be starting to feel like a living specimen.'

Noah drummed his fingers a bit impatiently on the counter-top. 'May I see the boy's notes, please?'

'Of course.' Anne proffered the file and Noah's eyes ran over the brief history.

'Fine.' He handed the file back to Anne. 'Now, with Dr Somers' approval, I'll have a chat with the parents and examine the boy.'

'I'll arrange a cup of tea for Mr and Mrs Bodetti, shall I?'

'Thanks, Anne,' Noah said. 'That would be an excellent idea. I'll send them out to you shortly.'

He was certainly very sure of himself. Erika stifled the twist of resentment as they made their way along the short corridor to the wards.

Joey Bodetti was the only patient in the three-bed unit. Clad only in pyjama bottoms, he was obviously bored, his eyes focusing in desultory fashion on the small television screen in front of him.

Taking in the tableau, Erika decided nothing short of a miracle would shift these parents from their son's bedside. Noah could well find himself as hamstrung as she'd been, even with the language barrier removed. She braced herself and went forward, her greeting to the family determinedly cheerful.

At the sound of her voice, Joey's head whipped

round, colour staining his youthful face. 'Hi, Dr Somers.'

He had a beautiful smile, Erika thought wryly. In fact, physically, he was a beautiful young man.

And he had a crush on her.

'Joey, this is Dr Jameson.' She stepped aside to allow Noah to come forward. 'He'd like to examine you and have a chat to your parents.'

In a flash the boy's Latin good looks turned sulky.

'Joey.' Noah nodded towards the boy, and in one all-encompassing inspection got the picture. He looked a question at Erika and then turned to the parents.

As he began to speak, Erika's hand went to her throat. She could only stand and stare as the Bodettis' indigenous language flowed from Noah's tongue.

It seemed the parents too were just as surprised. And almost overcome. Their rather solemn faces lit up like a laser show. 'Ah! *Dottore!*' Mr Bodetti grasped Noah by both arms, his relief palpable.

Quite quickly, Noah appeared to have all the information he needed, and then smoothly and gently he began ushering the parents from the room.

'Not feeling so hot, Joey?' Noah perched himself casually on his young patient's bed and raised a quizzical dark brow.

Joey remained stubbornly silent. I don't have to

talk to *you* clearly spelled out in the dismissive shrug of one shoulder.

Don't be a wretch, Joey, Erika pleaded silently. Wanting to help, she took a step forward.

Noah shot her a warning look and she faded reluctantly into the background.

'Want to tell me about it, Joey?'

Erika heard Noah's question, low-pitched, persuasive. Almost holding her breath, she watched Joey's young throat tighten with heartbreaking vulnerability, before he made faltering eye contact with the male doctor.

'I already talked to Dr Somers,' he dismissed. 'She's been great. Explained heaps of stuff.'

'I'm sure she has.' Noah didn't look at Erika. 'I hear you play soccer?'

'Yeah. And I'm good.'

Noah ignored the youthful brashness, asking, 'What position do you play?'

'I'm the striker.'

'Got a good turn of speed, have you?'

Joey looked up sharply, as though surprised at the calibre of the question. 'I can move a bit,' he said, warming slightly.

'I played keeper.' Noah's grin was slow and faintly reminiscent, and despite her misgivings Erika had to admire his touch—just enough of the proverbial mateship about him to get Joey to relax and trust him.

'You'd have had the height for it.' The boy's

head dipped shyly and he fiddled with his watchband. 'How far did you take it?'

'Oh, I played for the varsity team. Then I ran out of time.' Unhurriedly, Noah leaned forward, linking his hands across his knees. 'I guess you're hoping to turn professional one day?'

'That'd be cool.' Joey's smile flashed briefly. 'I could make mega-bucks.'

'Maybe you could,' Noah said, flicking a glance at his watch. 'Listen, mate, I've a date with Ted Campbell over at the garage to pick up my car, so how about you wriggle down flat for me now and we'll try to get a handle on what's bugging your system before I go? Good lad,' he approved, when Joey obliged like a lamb.

Erika left quietly.

CHAPTER TWO

AN INEXPLICABLE, alienating loneliness descended on her as she made her way back to the nurses' station.

'Noah coping?' Anne's smile never wavered.

Erika shrugged listlessly. 'Sorted out the parents in two minutes flat.'

'Hey there, you.' Anne reached out a comforting hand. 'Don't feel badly. All this is second nature to him now. And don't forget, this practice is Noah's livelihood. He does what he has to do.'

Erika made a small face. 'I must be feeling a bit thin-skinned today.'

'And I'll bet you skipped lunch.' Anne was already ushering her through to Sister's office. 'Take a pew and I'll see what the folks in the kitchen can rustle up.'

Erika owned to a feeling of mild desperation. She felt like some kind of lame duck, with Noah taking over her patient and now Anne, who was extremely busy in her own right, chasing up something as mundane as food for her.

Her nerves did feel a bit stretched, she admitted reluctantly, resting her forehead against the big picture window and looking pensively into the blue-green landscape of the valley below.

She'd had broken nights and a steady workload for the past month, yet neither had bothered her unduly before today. She sighed, lifting a hand to scoop the strands of hair away from her neck. It was Noah Jameson's sudden appearance and how it had affected her that was standing her equilibrium on its head...

'Here we are,' Anne announced cheerfully. 'Toasted cheese and tomato sandwiches and a pot of coffee. OK?'

'Oh, Anne, that's wonderful!' Erika felt her gastric juices react to the aroma of freshly brewed coffee. 'You shouldn't be waiting on me like this,' she protested. 'I could have gone along to the kitchen.'

'Rubbish,' Anne said mildly. 'Now, sit down and enjoy. Mugs in the top cupboard.'

Erika had munched her way steadily through all but two of the sandwiches and was on her second cup of coffee when Noah strolled in.

'Is that coffee?' he asked.

'Help yourself,' Erika said, watching him covertly, noting how his familiarity with the place lent a quiet air of certainty to his movements.

She swallowed. 'Well, what do you think? Is it RA?'

'No.'

'What, then?'

Noah hauled up another chair and sat opposite her. 'It's just a hunch yet. That's all it can be until we get the results of the blood test. But I think we're dealing with Lyme disease.'

Erika looked blank. Her faith in her diagnostic abilities tottered. Could she have been more aware, better informed? She'd thought she'd covered all the bases but apparently she hadn't. 'That's caused by a virus, isn't it?'

'Yes.' Noah's long fingers spanned his mug. 'It's tick-borne, carried in the parasite's saliva and toxic as all hell. And surprise, surprise,' he added drily, 'the Bodetti family has recently moved here from scrubby cattle country. It's my guess Joey's been bitten and his immune system has proven unequal to the toxin.'

Erika felt the nerves in her stomach tighten. 'He didn't mention any of that to me.'

'No.' Noah shot her a very dry smile. 'He was obviously distracted.'

'Noah—about that...' Erika's embarrassed gaze went to the floor.

'Hey, it happens.' Noah shrugged. 'The kid's a walking testosterone bank, and vulnerable.' He looked at her over the rim of his mug. 'As a matter of interest, how are you handling it?'

Erika felt the flush creep up her throat. 'In my own way, Noah. It'll mean a long course of antibiotics, won't it?' She skipped conversational channels quickly.

'Providing I'm right,' Noah qualified. 'When you were describing Joey's symptoms, it jogged my memory. Began to tie in with another case I treated here a couple of years ago.' He spread his arms on the table and leaned towards her.

Erika swallowed. The taut valley of tanned skin beneath his faded blue shirt was electrifying. The man just bristled with sex appeal. 'It's a pity we can't get the blood sample away earlier than Monday.'

'But we can.' Noah laid back in his chair, linking his hands behind his head. 'I've explained the position to the Bodettis in some detail. They're not short of money. They're quite happy for us to charter one of the local fly-boys to get the blood to Brisbane this afternoon.'

Erika felt the ground sliding out from under her. 'When you decide to move, you really move, don't you?'

'You're objecting?'

'I would have appreciated being included in your deliberations, certainly.'

He merely raised an eyebrow. 'Ticked off with me, aren't you, Erika? Because you've assumed I've hijacked your patient.'

'Did I say that?' Her brittle gaze flew up to meet his, to find his eyes running discerningly over her. She swallowed. She probably looked a mess. Her face hadn't seen make-up in days. There'd seemed no time, no reason...

'You didn't need to say anything,' he murmured, swinging to his feet. 'You realize I've looked over your day-sheets.' He was standing at the window, staring down into the valley much as she'd done earlier.

Erika moistened her lips. 'Aren't they in order?'

'Oh, quite. Congratulations.'

But he didn't sound as though he was congratulating her at all. Turning only his head, he eyed her broodingly, as though checking she really was the locum he'd employed four weeks ago. 'It's the extra things you've done that have me intrigued.'

'I don't understand—'

'No, I don't either,' he agreed with a similar kind of bewilderment. 'I can't believe the amount of personal time and energy you appear to have expended on some of my elderly patients.'

Erika's eyes blazed. 'I would've thought I was just doing my job.'

'Bunkum! Your sense of dedication terrifies me. And why risk burning yourself out for the sake of a list of patients you're not likely to see again? Why, Erika?' he repeated in soft puzzlement.

Her hand closed around the small medallion at her throat. Thoughts were spinning around in her head like leaves in a whirlwind. 'What's your point?'

He stared at her for a long moment. 'My point is, what brought you here, Erika? And don't tell me your reasons were altruistic. That I won't believe.'

'I don't care what you believe,' she returned sharply. 'And my reasons for coming here were personal. And frankly, Noah, I don't know why you're looking for a problem when there isn't one.'

'Have you been ill?'

'No!' Her voice was laced with frustration. She took a deep breath, looking up, relieved at the knock on the door.

Anne popped her head in. 'Thank goodness you're both still here. State Emergency's on the phone. A young lad's fallen on Mount Alford.'

'I'll speak,' Noah said calmly. 'Could you have the call put through here, please, Anne?'

Erika listened as Noah fired questions into the mouthpiece. There was probably a procedure they followed now, she thought. Obviously they wanted a doctor at the scene or they wouldn't have called the hospital. Mentally she began to prepare herself.

'That was Dirk Belzar from Rescue,' Noah said, clipping the receiver back into place. 'Apparently a young lad's gone off abseiling on his own and suffered the consequences.'

Erika's eyes widened in query. 'How far did he fall?'

Noah looked serious. 'Rolling and free falling about twenty metres.'

She suppressed a shudder. It was a wonder the boy hadn't been killed outright. 'What was it? Faulty anchor?'

'Appears so. The kid chose an unused route and then compounded matters by anchoring to a tree trunk. It gave way.'

'Poor kid...' Erika shook her head. 'How did Rescue know about him?'

'Mobile phone.' Noah ran his hand through his hair. 'But the message was a bit garbled, so either he's badly injured and passed out or he's done some damage to the phone in the fall.'

Either way, she had to get to him. Erika got quickly to her feet. 'What do I have to do?'

'Nothing.' Noah's voice was firm. 'I'll go.'

'You're on leave,' she said, as if that was an end to the matter. 'And if we're going to get pedantic, I'm the MO in charge at the moment.'

'And I still call the shots,' he countered. 'Besides...' his dark brows beetled together '...the terrain around Mount Alford is extremely hazardous.'

'Meaning what, exactly?' Erika could hardly contain her disbelief. 'I'm a reasonably capable person, Noah. I've trekked in the highlands of New Guinea. I've some idea of mountains.' She made her tone heavy with satire, her eyes lit with quiet determination.

Noah's eyes tracked his locum's pale, set face. 'Can you abseil?'

Her throat lumped. Did that mean she'd have to actually descend to where the boy was injured? She felt a stab of panic, and then her chin came up. 'I've done a bit.'

'OK.' Noah held up his hands in mock surrender. 'It will certainly lessen the risks with two of us. But I don't want any heroics, Doctor,' he warned. 'Be prepared to do what I tell you.'

Erika raged inwardly. The man's arrogance was beyond belief!

'We'll take a retrieval kit with us,' he said, picking up the phone and concentrating on dialling a number. 'Anne should have it ready by now. If you could chase it up? I'll be with you in a minute.'

'Anything I can do?' Erika asked, finding the charge nurse in the nearby utility room.

'Just about ready.' Anne gave a wry smile. 'Climbing's practically a religion around here. We more or less keep everything on standby. There, that should just about do it, I think.' She stepped back from the bench. 'Now, if you'll just hang on a tick, I'll get the emergency drugs from the fridge.'

Erika watched the young woman go. Anne was a gem, she thought. Bright and intuitive, and with loads of common sense. For a fleeting moment Erika wondered about Anne Bryson's private life. She was barely thirty and already a widow, her police officer husband having been fatally shot on duty several years previously. And now Anne had the sole responsibility of rearing the couple's six-year-old daughter, Holly...

'All set?' Noah appeared at the door.

Erika jerked back to the present, her hands gripping the benchtop behind her. 'Anne's just gone for the drugs.' Her eyes clouded with faint uncertainty. 'Um—how far to this Mount Alford?'

'About a twenty-minute drive.' He moved round

beside her so that their arms were almost touching. 'Second thoughts, Erika?'

Her lips contracted into a little moue of studied patience. 'You don't have to worry about me, Noah. I'm fine.'

'Liar,' he countered very softly. 'You're scared witless. If I didn't think it's going to take expertise from both of us, I wouldn't let you within a mile of this retrieval.'

She gazed at him in disbelief. 'You have to be joking! I'm not some airhead!'

He shrugged. 'Nothing personal. I don't want two casualties on my hands, that's all.'

For a brief, mind-numbing second, she toyed with the idea of kicking him in the shins, but then Anne providentially arrived. Tight-lipped, Erika put the action on hold—but not before she'd decided that being a locum was sometimes the absolute pits.

'Thanks, Anne,' Noah acknowledged, stowing the drugs pack carefully and hefting the gear. 'Keep in touch by mobile, hmm?' He smiled down at the charge. 'So far, so good. The CareFlight chopper's on its way from Brisbane.'

Anne nodded. 'Mind how you both go.'

'What's the plan?' Erika paused with her hand on the ignition.

Noah clamped his seatbelt. 'Drop me at the garage. We'll take my vehicle. Then go to your flat and change into something more serviceable. Jeans and a long-sleeved shirt. And shoes, if you have them.' He looked pointedly at her grey suede loafers on the pedals. 'And I don't mean the ones you'd wear to the races, Erika.'

She widened her eyes innocently before she ignited the motor. 'I'll bring my bonnet and shawl too. Just to be on the safe side.'

Noah snorted and looked at his watch.

Erika tugged on her jeans, cursing and almost falling over in her haste. 'Damn!' she breathed wrathfully. Seven minutes, he'd said. And all her long-sleeved shirts were in the wash. She blew out a calming breath and dug out the only other alternative, a canary-yellow sweatshirt. At least they'd see her coming! She tugged it over her head.

She thought about the descent itself, recognising the flutter in her stomach. It wasn't fear, exactly, but certainly nerves. She hadn't done any real exercise for an age. Please heaven she'd have enough all-round physical fitness to get through.

Dirk Belzar from the rescue squad was waiting for them at the mountain-top, tall and athletic. His fair hair looked almost golden in the last of the sun's rays.

'It'll be no holiday camp,' he said grimly. 'You won't have much room to move on that ledge.' He looked a bit rueful. 'I'd like to come with you, but I'm needed here to co-ordinate the air-lift. We're a bit short on personnel today.'

'We'll manage.' Noah was shrugging on a close-fitting navy jumper. 'Won't we?' He tipped a meaningful look at Erika.

'All it needs is teamwork, Noah.' And a good dose of skill and courage, she added silently, bending to select one of the lightweight safety helmets from Dirk's gear and tugging it over her hair.

Seconds later they were climbing into their harness. 'I've used the figure-of-eight knot,' Dirk explained to Erika. 'OK?'

'That's the one I'm used to.' She smiled briefly, testing the rope, settling it between her jeans-clad legs and under her right thigh.

'The wind's come up.' Dirk rested his hand fleetingly on her shoulder. 'Take it easy on the way down, yeah?'

Noah could hardly contain his impatience. Deliberately, he strode up to Erika and tapped her on the shoulder. 'If you're quite ready?'

'I'm ready.' Her eyes flickered.

'I'll lead,' he informed her brusquely, and slipped over the edge.

Bouncing down the granite face of the mountain, Erika kept a firm hold on her abseiling rope. She was out of practice. There were no two ways about it. But then the descent was hardly a piece of cake. She just hoped Noah knew where they were going.

'You OK?' he called to her from time to time, as they payed out the rope and went down, down.

'Fine.' Erika's teeth were clamped. Adrenalin was pumping out of her and sweat rippled across her forehead and sat stickily at the base of her neck. She didn't dare look down. Even knowing they were secured didn't help her trepidation. The drop was fearsome.

Finally they were down. Erika landed with a little thump. Turning sharply, she almost cannoned into Noah's chest.

'Steady!' His thumbs bit briefly into her upper arms. 'Sure you're OK?'

'A bit shaky there for a while,' she admitted breathily. 'I'm woefully out of practice.'

'I wouldn't say that…'

She blinked in confusion. His soft words had taken her by surprise. Sent out a definite message. Her thoughts scrambled. 'Which way now?'

Noah squinted into the sun, then let her go. 'According to Dirk we should begin to move roughly twenty or so metres to our left around this craggy outfall. That should bring us to our patient. Stay close to me.'

Confused, Erika stayed glued to the spot. Her knees felt ready to give out at any minute, and it had nothing to do with the descent they'd just made. She squeezed her eyes shut but the sensual images wouldn't go away.

'Erika?' Noah touched her shoulder and she turned instantly to him. 'We need to get on,' he said, his voice clipped.

Erika soon realised even for the experienced the going was difficult and narrow, fraught with the unexpected.

'Watch out for stuff like this. There's no foothold,' Noah warned, testing his boot against a huge grass root. Disturbed, the clump gave way easily, revealing a sparse, thready root system.

Erika stilled, feeling perspiration lodge wetly in the small of her back. 'We should've had a week's preparation to prepare mentally for a jaunt like this.'

'Don't look down, if it's a problem,' Noah said.

'It isn't,' she insisted. 'Oh—' She ran hard up against him when he stopped abruptly. 'What is it?'

Noah frowned. 'According to my reckoning, the boy should be round about here.'

But he wasn't. Erika's nerves tightened. Had they come the wrong way? And would it mean retracing their steps along that tortuous ledge? Heavens, she hoped not!

'Listen!' Noah's head went up and he stilled.

Erika could hear something between a moan and a whimper, and definitely human.

'The lad must have got himself into a cave or something.' Noah was already inching further. 'Will you be OK with this, Erika?'

'I'll manage.' She gave a cracked laugh. Her legs felt as loose as a puppet's and there was a crick in her neck. But she couldn't tell Noah that. She'd already sensed he possessed the mental discipline of a skilled climber, and physically, powerfully built and all, he was as sure-footed as a mountain goat.

They continued to push forward slowly, painstakingly. Erika dared a glance downwards into the blue-purple valley. 'Ooh—' She pressed into the cliff-face while her stomach heaved and did a ninety-degree turn.

Noah swore under his breath. Again that unfamiliar stab of protectiveness surged into his body. 'Take some deep breaths,' he instructed, placing his hands firmly on her shoulders. His mouth drew in. 'Maybe you weren't up to this after all.'

Nettled, she shrugged out from under his hold. 'I'm fine, Noah. And you did say it would be better with two of us,' she reminded him sharply.

'That's beside the point.' His gaze flinted. 'I'm a trained member of the rescue team. If it came to it, I could have managed on my own. Now, if we've sorted that out, we'd better keep moving. Warn me if you're about to throw up, OK?'

Charming! Erika made a face at his broad back and retired into dignified silence.

The sounds of human distress magnified, leading them directly to the cave. 'Mind your head,' he cautioned, bending slightly to enter.

Erika followed, peering into the gloom beyond. The cave seemed to have an odour about it, she thought, but at least it appeared dry.

'Hello-o!' Noah's call echoed eerily into the cavernous space. A muffled cry came back. 'Bloody hell!' He reeled back as something dark and winged brushed past.

'Aagh!' Erika made an ineffectual swipe at the air. 'Fruit bats?'

'Probably a colony of them,' Noah agreed. 'They'll be going out to feed as soon as it's dusk. Let's not hang around any longer than we need to. We'll try this corridor over here.' Taking Erika's arm, he kept her close to his side. 'And there's our boy,' he murmured with satisfaction, and simultaneously they saw the huddled form just inside the entrance.

'It's OK, son.' Noah's voice was reassuring. Slipping the emergency kit off his shoulders, he hunkered down beside the boy. 'I'm Noah and this is Erika,' he said calmly. 'We're doctors. What's your name?'

CHAPTER THREE

'JASON—I'm hurt bad...' The boy sucked air in through trembling lips and cast fearful eyes at his rescuers. 'Leg...' he groaned.

Erika felt her heart lurch as she dropped beside Noah, seeing at a glance the irregularity of the lad's right leg. It was several centimetres shorter than the other, and now sat painfully out of joint. Dear God, the pain he must be in. She looked to Noah. 'Fractured NOF?'

'Looks like it. Get us some light, would you, please? Take it easy now, son.' Noah gently lifted the youth's head and applied the oxygen mask, while Erika unzipped a section of the emergency kit, finding the torch. She activated it, sending a powerful beam of light around their patient.

Noah flicked his stethoscope over the boy's chest. 'Breathing's not too bad,' he murmured, laying the stethoscope to one side. Carefully, he began palpating the youth's stomach.

Erika knew he'd be checking for any sign of hardening that would indicate internal bleeding. 'I'll get a line in,' she said, whipping a tourniquet around Jason's arm. 'That's if I can,' she qualified, tapping urgently to prompt a vein to the surface.

All her trauma training came rushing back, as

vividly as the rays of setting sun outside the cave. She clamped her lips, frowning. Jason's loss of blood could be pre-empting shock. This is all we need, she gritted silently, for his veins to begin their automatic protective response, conserving blood for the heart, lungs and brain.

'Come on...' she breathed. 'Give a little. Got it!' Letting her breath go in relief, she slid the cannula into the boy's vein.

'Clever girl,' Noah murmured.

'Lucky.' She fended off the compliment with a taut smile.

'Lucky and clever.' Noah's hand tightened on her shoulder, his gaze going back to their patient. 'There's not much of him. Let's go with ten milligrams of Maxolon and five of morphine. We'll follow with fifty of pethidine. That should get him through transportation to the hospital.'

'Are you allergic to anything that you know of, Jason?' Erika asked, preparing to administer the painkiller.

Eyes dulled with pain, the youngster shook his head.

'Hang in there, mate.' Noah let his hand rest briefly on the boy's fair head. 'Dr Somers is giving you some medication to lessen the pain, OK? You'll be on your way to hospital pretty soon.' He looked at Erika. 'Ready?'

She nodded, quickly swabbing the cannula and shooting the first two drugs home, praying the injection would work and soon.

'Watch him.' Noah's voice was clipped. He began pulling himself upright. 'I'll start splinting. The sooner we get him on that retrieval stretcher and air-lifted out of this place, the better.'

Teamwork, Erika thought thankfully. That was what she'd said they needed, and without doubt that was exactly what they had. Their movements, even their thoughts, were dovetailing without effort.

'How's he doing?' Noah's sharp question broke into her musing.

'Breathing's easier.' She scrambled to her feet. 'He's beginning to relax.' She watched as Noah placed the supportive splints between the boy's legs. 'Bandages?'

'Please. Unless you intend tearing up your shirt?'

'I will if you will,' she quipped drily, digging out the thick bandages they'd need to bind Jason's injured leg to his good one.

Working swiftly and co-operatively, they had him secured within seconds and ready to be placed on the collapsible CareFlight stretcher.

'Right.' Noah glanced at his watch. 'So far so good. I'll have to go back to the entrance now, to use the mobile. I'll call Dirk. The chopper should be arriving any time now.' He looked down at Jason's still form. 'I should think you could administer that shot of pethidine now, Erika.'

When he'd gone, Erika beat back a feeling of isolation. Which was crazy, she thought. Now that they knew the layout of the cave, Noah's mission would take hardly any time at all.

'Hell...' she murmured, feeling spooked. The bats had started up their chittering as they fought for positions in the nooks and crevices of the cave.

Erika took herself to task. She had a job to do. Give Jason the pethidine. About to draw up the dose, she stopped and froze. Something was wrong here.

Dreadfully wrong.

'No-aah!' Her cry echoed and re-echoed, bouncing off the walls of the cave.

Jason was gulping, his eyes rolling back in his head, his colour grey. Erika shuddered. In a few seconds, if she didn't act, he'd be blue.

In a flash her training had smothered her fear. In one swift movement, she ripped Jason's shirt open and began chest compressions.

Noah's bulk dropped beside her. 'What's happened?' he barked.

'He's throwing a PE!'

Noah's expletive hit the ceiling. He grabbed for the life-saving equipment. He would have to intubate. A pulmonary embolism. Damn! He should have seen it coming, he berated himself. All the ingredients were there. A serious fracture. Fat escaping from the break, gumming up the arteries. Damn, damn and double damn!

Gently, skilfully, he passed the tube down Jason's trachea, attaching it to the oxygen. 'Breathe,' he grated. 'Come on!'

Erika bit her lips together. With sickening dread she swung her gaze and watched Noah check and re-check the carotid pulse in the boy's neck. He shook his head.

'We'll have to zap him.' Noah's voice roughened. 'I'll get the life-pack. We're not losing him after all this effort.'

Erika longed to ease her neck and shoulders, but there was no time for that luxury. She had to keep the compressions going. Choice would be a fine thing, she thought, almost light-headed, feeling the perspiration patch wetly across her forehead.

'Noah—hurry—' Erika found herself trying to breathe for the boy.

Noah got into position. 'Be ready to take over the bag when I defibrillate,' he snapped.

Erika kept her mind focused. Jason's life could depend on their teamwork now.

'OK, now!'

Almost in slow motion she reached out and took over the air viva bag.

'And clear!'

Erika dropped the bag and spun back, praying that the volts of electricity would do their job and start the heart's rhythm.

'Nothing,' Noah muttered. 'Let's go to two hundred. And clear!'

Pale and tight-lipped, Erika let her gaze swing to the monitor. She swallowed jerkily. The trace was still flat.

'Damn!' Noah dragged in a breath that hollowed

his cheeks. 'Start compressions again, Erika,' he snapped. 'I'm giving him adrenalin. We're running out of options here.'

'We can't give up—'

Noah's mouth firmed into a thin line. His fingers curled around the mini-jet, already prepared with its life-giving dose of adrenalin. With swift precision he slid the long needle neatly between Jason's ribs and into his heart.

'We are not going to lose you, Jason,' he grated, wiping the sweat from his forehead with his forearm. 'Hear me? Clear.' He activated the charge and their combined gazes swung to the monitor.

'Yes!' Noah roared. 'We've done it, Erika! You beauty!'

Erika felt her mouth trembling uncontrollably, swallowing the tears of reaction that ran unashamedly down her cheeks. Hastily, she blinked them away, holding her hands against her eyes, gathering her composure.

'Erika! Hey...' Noah's arm came around her shoulders, hugging her. 'Don't cry. We've got him back.'

'Oh! I—yes, I know...' she said huskily, turning her head away. She beat back the last of the tears and swallowed. 'Noah—he's waking up.'

Their young patient was indeed waking up, panic and distress in his eyes.

'It's OK, Jase.' Erika bent to reassure him. 'You'll be fine,' she murmured, rubbing warmth into his hand. 'Dr Jameson just worked a small miracle.'

'With a little help from my friend,' Noah growled, a deep cleft between his dark brows.

Erika drew in a deep breath. She felt hollowed out. They'd come so close to losing Jason. She turned to Noah, chewing her lip. 'I'd like to give him ten milligrams of midazolam now, Doctor. Do you agree?'

Noah's mouth quirked into a wry smile. 'Absolutely,' he said.

'Hello, in there! Noah?'

'Ah!' Noah's dark head went back. 'Sounds like Butch Cassidy from the chopper squad's here.'

Erika clicked her tongue. 'He was never christened *Butch*! What's his real name?' she whispered as the man's rangy figure came into view.

One eyebrow lifted. 'Barry. Not nearly so impressive, is it? This is my locum, Erika Somers, Butch,' Noah said as they shook hands.

'G'day, Doc.' There was a smile in Butch's voice. 'Thrown you in at the deep end, has he?'

'And as you see I've survived.' Erika looked a challenge at Noah. 'Pleased to meet you, Butch.'

'Hey, likewise.' Butch rubbed his chin. 'You here for much longer?'

'About another week…' Noah cleared his throat and her gaze faltered. They'd shared something here today. Something so intense it had momentarily laid bare their emotions.

She saw Noah's dark brows flex in query and

realised she'd been staring. 'Jason's asleep,' she deflected quickly, turning to Butch. 'Could we move him now?'

'Ready when you are, Doc.'

'You'll need to keep a close eye on him,' Noah warned. 'We've intubated and sedated him and he's back in sinus rhythm. But he could go again.'

Big Butch Cassidy was no novice to the job. He knew well the battle that had been fought here and for the moment won. 'We'll watch him, Doc. No worries.'

'On my count, then,' Noah said, and in unison they gently rolled Jason first on one side and then the other, sliding each section of the supporting plinth under him and snapping the pieces together.

Outside the cave the CareFlight helicopter was waiting, its rotors beating the air, as it hovered. And below it, attached by sturdy ropes, the basket-like orange-coloured cradle dangled, waiting to receive the stretcher bearing the injured boy.

'OK, who's coming?' Butch's bright blue gaze tracked between the two medics and he held out the extra harness.

'You go,' Noah said brusquely, helping Erika into the harness. 'Well done,' he murmured, and bent to load the life-pack on to the stretcher.

'Back for you shortly, Noah.' Butch gave the thumbs-up sign and the ascent began slowly and carefully to the top.

The helicopter was gone, circling, banking and then heading towards the coast. Looking up, Erika tracked its flight across the pale sky until it disappeared into the fluffy pink clouds. She felt a surge of relief. They'd done all they could and now Jason was on his way to specialist medical treatment.

'Dirk's about to take off back to base.' Noah touched her shoulder.

'Oh—' She tugged the safety helmet off her head and ran her fingers through her flattened hair. 'I'd better return this, then.'

'Thanks for your efforts today, folks.' Dirk stowed the last of his gear in the emergency vehicle and slammed the rear door. He turned and shook hands with them. 'Nice result.'

'Let's hope so.' Noah was guarded.

The air was quiet again after Dirk had taken off down the mountain road. 'Are you in a hurry to get back?' Noah asked, smiling slightly.

For reasons she couldn't explain, her heart quickened. 'No—I—why?'

'The view from the lookout is quite spectacular.'

'Where will they take Jason?' she asked, doing her best to keep up with his long strides.

'Ambrose Memorial. They have an excellent orthopaedic team there.'

'I'd like to keep tabs on him.'

'That shouldn't be a problem.' Noah stopped suddenly and stared at her. She took everything so much to heart… 'I was wrong earlier,' he said, his blue eyes darkening. 'I couldn't have managed without you.'

She blinked uncertainly. 'I'm sure neither of us has done a course in miracles, Noah. We did what we had to do.'

His mouth folded in on a smile. 'You're a fine doctor, Erika Somers.'

She flushed. 'As you are, Noah.' Her slender arms closed around her body as if to protect it, her uneasy suspicion of their mutual attraction firming.

But there could be no future in it. She shook her head as if to clear it. In a few days she'd be gone. Stricken by the realisation, she took a step forward. 'You—um—mentioned a view?'

Erika's strange unease was soon lost in the magnificence of the view. And safely behind the guard rail she could take her fill, breathe in its very essence.

'I've always thought this place was pretty special,' Noah said quietly.

'The high country of Victoria is incredibly beautiful,' she allowed, something wistful in her tone. 'But this...' Words seemed to elude her. Instead she swept her hand across the vastness in front of them.

The view was neverending. Timeless. Hazed in the blue-purple of afternoon, the air crisp, glassily still with the departing rays of the sun.

'Oh, Noah...' She tipped her head up to the sky.

The sharp ting-ting echoed from the valley floor. 'Bellbird.' Noah smiled across at her. 'Want to try a coo-ee?' His hands cupped his mouth to give the Australian bush call.

'Don't. Don't break the spell.' Erika shook her head. 'Please…' Slightly overcome, she turned to him. The wind had lifted his dark hair and his shirt collar was all askew under the navy jumper. He looked so alive! So physical she wanted to reach out and touch him. *Stroke* him. Their gazes meshed and she felt a faint heat come to her skin.

'Erika…?' Noah caught her about the waist.

Her eyes dilated and she shivered beneath his hands. 'What—?' She swallowed. 'What are you doing?'

'Just this,' he husked, gathering her into his arms and cradling her against the solidness of his chest.

A brief whimper of disbelief escaped from her mouth and then her hands were sliding under his jumper until her arms were around him, anchoring him as if she'd never let him go.

Her lips were against his throat, and she had the wildest need to open her mouth. To taste him and be tasted in return.

'Erika?' His voice was a murmur against her lips until his mouth caught her own breathy sigh, swallowing it, savouring it, until he claimed her fully, with a passion that shook her to the core.

Then just as suddenly it was over. Like a fever that had passed.

'Oh—' Erika exhaled a ragged little breath and

buried her face in his chest, breathing in the warm male closeness of him like life-saving oxygen.

Somehow they got back to his Land Rover.

'Dirk left us a flask of coffee.' Noah seemed to have trouble with his voice.

'That was nice of him. Oh, hell...' Erika sank on to the ground and pulled her knees up to her chin. Keeping her eyes downcast, she accepted the hot drink from Noah's outstretched hand. 'What was that all about, do you suppose?' she asked huskily, and knew she was asking herself as much as him.

Noah settled beside her. 'Does there have to be a reason?' His voice was soft, slightly gravelly.

They drank their coffee in silence, shifting back against the front of his vehicle, using the sturdy bull-bars for support.

'You look shattered.' Noah finally broke the silence. 'Why don't we get together for dinner this evening? Relax a bit.'

In a quick, protective movement, Erika put her hand to her mouth, feeling his kiss return in a wash of quivering nerve-ends. 'I should get some sleep, actually. There may be a call-out—'

'I'll do your calls,' he said equably. 'In fact...' he tipped her chin up with a finger. 'Why don't you take the rest of the weekend off? I'll cover the morning surgery on Monday as well.'

'That hardly fulfils my contract.' Erika looked doubtful. 'You're the one supposed to be on holiday.'

'Don't argue with me, Dr Somers.' Noah let his gaze wander over the creamy perfection of her skin, the full, just-kissed mouth, resisting the urge to kiss her again. 'So,' he asked softly. 'Do we have a dinner date?'

'Noah—' Erika heard the slightly desperate note in her voice and winced. 'Honestly, you don't have to do this.'

Noah gave a shrug. 'What's wrong with two colleagues having a meal together? Do you have a problem with that?'

Make it a thousand, she thought, with the kind of uncertainty she was feeling around him. She bit her lip. 'All right, then.' She shrugged her capitulation. 'As long as we don't eat Italian.'

Noah's dark brows shot up. 'You don't like Italian food?'

'Too much, probably.' Erika bit back a smile. 'But it seems to me half the population of Hillcrest have Italian ancestry, and half of those again have opened restaurants. I think I may have overdosed on pasta and everything that goes with it,' she confessed.

'What?' He frowned. 'Takeaways?'

She nodded.

'For a month?'

'Every night—almost.'

'Good grief!' Noah shook his head and with a decisive movement pulled out his mobile phone.

'This calls for dining out in style,' he declared, giving her a teasing smile. 'And I know just the place. Great atmosphere and not too rowdy, even on a Saturday night.'

'Noah—' Erika tried to put a brake on his light-hearted game. 'There's really no need to go to all this trouble. I'd be quite happy with an old-fashioned roast dinner at the pub.'

'Trust me, Erika. I know exactly what you need. My friends Marianne and Rob operate a great little eatery just out of town. I'll give them a call. Ask them to reserve a table for us.' He began whistling under his breath, clearly engrossed in his plan.

Erika watched his long fingers punch out the numbers and her heart lurched. He sat there so male, so pleased with the idea of giving her a treat.

He put the phone to his ear, setting teasing blue eyes on her as the number answered. 'Hey, Roberto!' His voice carried on the still air. *'Come sta?'*

Erika gaped, her eyes widening in laughing disbelief. He wouldn't! Would he?

What should she wear? Erika sifted through the possibilities, finally deciding on pale linen pants and a gold camisole top. A faint excitement began to build in the pit of her stomach as she laid the clothes across the bed.

She was ready and waiting a few minutes before Noah's appointed time to call for her. 'I'm feeling almost glamorous,' she told her reflection in the long mirror.

Noah was right on time. Hastily smoothing a

hand down the back of her hair, she went to let him in, sharply aware her mouth was too dry, her heart beating way too fast.

'Noah...' she blinked out into the soft light, trying not to stare. He was casually but elegantly dressed in grey trousers, a darker grey jacket of a distinctive tweed, and a soft white shirt open at the throat, emphasising his olive-toned skin.

'Not too early, am I?' He flashed her a smiling query.

'No.' She motioned him inside. 'I'm quite ready.'

'You look a million dollars.' His blue eyes flinted briefly. 'But won't you need a jacket or something?'

'Um—I have one somewhere.' She looked around, disconcerted. For some reason Noah's compliment had made her feel vulnerable, and as uninitiated as a schoolgirl.

'Is this what you're looking for?' He held up the little cropped jacket, his expression softening as he draped it around her. 'Ready?' He tipped her a lopsided smile and, tucking her hand through his arm, he swept her outside into the starry night.

He was silent as they drove, and Erika glanced several times at his still profile before she asked, 'I guess it's too soon to have had any news of Jason?'

'Funny you should ask.' Noah concentrated on swinging his Land Rover out on to the open road. 'As a matter of fact I rang my contact at the

Ambrose a short while ago. The chopper arrived safely and Jason's been admitted. They hope to operate within the next couple of hours.'

Erika felt the weight of responsibility lift from her. 'I imagine Butch would have been relieved to hand him over to the medical team.'

'Mmm. But apparently he starred in his own small drama as well. It seems our Jason is a top-line apprentice jockey in Brisbane. A news crew from one of the TV networks was waiting for the chopper to arrive.'

'What on earth could have made him do something so crazy?' Erika wondered aloud. 'And why choose this part of the world in which to do it? It's obvious he wasn't an experienced climber.'

'No, he wasn't,' Noah said. 'So I delved a bit. I thought we were entitled to some explanation, given the whole escapade almost cost the kid his life. It seems our Jason had a row with his boss and just took off. Hitched a ride to Hillcrest. He knew the place from holidays as a youngster.'

'Poor kid.' Erika shook her head. 'Maybe he just wanted to get something out of his system.'

'Chose a dangerous way of doing it, then.' Noah was sceptical. 'But I guess when you're as young as Jason problems can seem insurmountable.'

And not only when you're young, Erika reflected wryly, looking down at her hands clasped neatly on her lap. And there was still a shadow of uncertainty in her eyes as Noah parked in front of the restaurant.

'Well, this is Peaches,' he told her, arcing a hand towards the softly lit stone-washed building.

'Cute name.' Erika released her seatbelt and smiled across at him.

'Oh—this is absolutely charming!' In the restaurant Erika gazed around her, turning and turning, her eyes lapping up the decor.

'You should see your face.' Grinning, Noah took her hand, leading her towards the stocky, dark-haired man bearing down on them. 'Here's Rob,' he said.

Erika blinked, her smile widening as the two men shook hands and good-naturedly thumped one another across the shoulders. Finally, Noah drew her to his side.

'Rob, this is Erika Somers, my locum.'

'Hi, Erika.' Rob's handshake was firm. 'I've caught the odd glimpse of you around town. It's good to meet you at last.'

'And you, Rob.' Erika's gaze flicked to the bright geranium growing happily from an earthenware pot. 'You have a lovely restaurant.'

'Thanks.' He looked pleased. 'Marianne's inspiration mostly.'

'Speaking of your beautiful wife.' Noah's enquiring gaze swept the precincts. 'Where is she?'

Rob's hand flexed backwards. 'Putting the final touches to your roast, I believe. Come, I have your table ready.' He spread his arms in an ushering gesture, taking them through to a kind of conservatory complete with glass walls and ceiling. He pointed upwards. 'Nice night for stargazing.'

Rob saw Erika seated and then looked across at his friend. 'What'll you have to drink, mate?'

Noah had no particular preference. 'A nice local red?'

'Got just the one.' Rob beamed and left them.

Noah's mouth quirked. 'I had you going there for a while.'

'Maybe for a minute this afternoon.' Erika's mouth tilted, a bubble of laughter rising in her throat. 'Anyhow, Rob's spilt the beans now. We're having a roast, by all accounts.'

'Got to keep my locum happy.'

Erika's heart thumped. He sat there looking as pleased as if he'd won the pools, and she realised for the first time in ages she felt truly in tune with her world.

With their wine sampled and poured, Noah raised his glass. 'To us, I think.'

'To us,' she echoed, adding silently, Whatever that might mean in the long run...

They made desultory conversation for a while, until Noah said, 'Now, if I'm covering, what should I know?'

Erika took a relieved breath. This was safer ground. 'Actually...' She gave him a rueful smile. 'I think Tara Petani has her dates wrong.'

'Oh, brilliant.' His voice was dry. 'Are you telling me I can expect to be called out tonight?'

'It's a possibility.' Erika acknowledged the smiling waitress who brought their soup. 'I examined her on Thursday. The baby seemed to be settling itself nicely to join the world. And sooner rather than later.'

'Well, from my recollection it seemed to be progressing nicely weight-wise,' Noah said. 'So we shouldn't have a problem even if she is early.' He sent Erika a lopsided grin. 'Want to come in and give me a hand if it happens tonight?'

'Indian giver,' she chided softly. 'I'm off duty. Remember?'

'Ah—yes.' He smiled, a mere sensual curving of his lips. 'Agreeable kind of chap, aren't I?' He refilled her wineglass but took only water for himself. 'Anyone else you want to confer about?'

'Mmm.' Erika took a piece of Marianne's homemade bread. 'Bert Hallam.'

Noah snorted. 'That old rogue. He'd try the patience of a saint.'

'He's been through two World Wars,' Erika said pointedly. 'He's entitled to.'

'Don't tell me he's got under your skin, Dr Somers?'

Erika concentrated on her soup. 'He's a lonely old man. Highly intelligent when you get past the gruff exterior. I arranged with the State Library to send him some history books.'

'I heard.' Noah's tone was softly amused. 'So, what's his current problem?'

'His feet need attention. Does the district boast such a person as a visiting podiatrist?'

'Afraid not. But I guess there's nothing stopping us from trying to find someone. And if there were enough prospective clients...'

'I'll work something out with Jenny.' Erika's face was alive with purpose. 'Like a survey form. And we could leave some around the surgery and at the shops. What do you think?'

Noah met her eyes steadily. 'I think I wonder how I ever managed without you.'

CHAPTER FOUR

ERIKA felt awkward under what amounted to fulsome praise. 'I can quite see why you needed a holiday,' she sidetracked swiftly. 'The area you cover is a big responsibility for a sole practitioner.'

'Mmm.' Noah's lips twitched thoughtfully. 'Perhaps we should talk about that. Anyone special waiting for your return to Melbourne, Erika?'

'Family,' she said, deliberately misinterpreting his question. 'Parents, brothers, sister-in-law.'

His eyebrows rose slightly. 'Can I assume, then, you're at liberty to make a lifestyle decision? Or is there a boyfriend, fiancé, whomever, you need to consider?'

'There's Alistair,' she said quietly.

'And where does he fit in exactly?' Noah asked, lifting his glass and taking a mouthful of water.

Erika shrugged. 'We've known one another for years. He was at university with my brother, Dean. His people are in the country, so he often came to us for weekends, the odd Christmas...'

'Are you living together?'

She shook her head. 'But he's been asking me for ages to marry him.'

'And are you going to?'

'Perhaps...' Her hand shook slightly as she

lifted her glass and took a mouthful of wine. 'He's a special person. And nice too.'

Noah snorted. 'So is my grandmother! You don't marry someone because they're *nice!*'

Erika sent him a tight smile. 'Why does one marry someone, then, Noah? What's the special ingredient?'

'Passion.' Their eyes met, and there was a sudden stillness between them.

Suddenly, Erika could feel herself flushing. Passion was the last thing she'd apply to her relationship with Alistair. But there was warmth there. And compatibility...

'Sorry.' Noah's slow smile warmed the space between them. 'I must sound like a right know-it-all.'

She shook her head. He sounded like a man who knew exactly what he wanted from a relationship. 'Why aren't you married?' The words popped out before she could stop them.

He coloured faintly. 'I wanted to be. Expected to be. It didn't work out,' he added, looking broodingly past her into the distance.

Erika sensed their shared relief when their roast dinner arrived. Moments later, and quite naturally, she said, 'You know, it concerns me you have no humidicrib.'

Noah's expression closed thoughtfully. 'Don't think it hasn't occurred to me. And any mum who's looking a bit suspect I refer over to the district hospital in Warwick in plenty of time. But in actual fact acquiring a humidicrib is down as a priority when we have our next fundraiser.'

Erika's eyes widened with interest. 'What things do you normally do to raise money?'

'Nothing too adventurous.' Noah's mouth turned down. 'It's hard to raise funds in a small community. The locals get fed up with calls on their hard-earned dollar, and bored with the same old raffles and street stalls.' He sent her a twisted smile. 'Perhaps we need a glamour event.'

'What about a festival?' Erika suggested. 'Or more precisely an Italian festival.'

Noah looked mildly amused. 'We'd need to attract people from everywhere to make anything like that a goer, Erika. Hillcrest doesn't have the population of Melbourne.'

'Well, I think it's your answer.' She refused to be daunted. 'The food alone would draw lots of people. And surely one of the city motor dealers could be persuaded to exhibit a few Italian racing cars in a good cause. And bikes,' she considered as an afterthought.

'Motorbikes?'

'Why not?' She ignored his hoot of laughter. 'Show me the young guy who can resist the pull of a Ducati. All that new leather and sleek bodywork. And if they came to see the bikes, they'd naturally spend their money on food and other attractions at the festival.'

An indulgent smile played around Noah's mouth. 'So, OK. We've lined up the food, fast cars and motorbikes. What else would draw the crowds?'

She flashed him a triumphant grin. 'Italian musicians.'

'Pavarotti?'

'Now you're taking the mickey.' Her downcast lashes fanned darkly across her cheekbones. 'Seriously, Noah, if you want to raise money for a humidicrib, the idea has possibilities.'

'You've really taken this community to your heart, haven't you?' He spoke gravely, leaning across to trap her hand between his palm and the starched linen of the tablecloth.

Erika felt her pulse rocketing at the intimacy. 'Do—you have a committee?' she forced out jerkily.

'We do.' Noah released her hand and she was stricken by the sense of loss. 'And you're changing the subject. The practice would carry two of us, Erika.'

She bit her lip. 'Are you—asking me to stay on here?'

'I'm asking you to think about it,' he said, his blue eyes fixed on her. 'Perhaps the idea, like your festival, has distinct possibilities.'

Perhaps it did, but she couldn't think about it now. If she accepted Noah's offer there would be huge repercussions—from Alistair, from her family. Especially from her father. 'What's this vegetable?' she deflected swiftly. 'It tastes very sweet.'

'Yam,' Noah said shortly. 'It's being grown

commercially now. Although I'm told our indigenous people have been eating it in its wild state for ever. Is the meal to your liking?'

'Superb.' Erika raised her glass and smiled at him across the rim. 'We must thank Marianne before we leave.'

'Perhaps she and Rob will have time to have coffee with us.' Noah went quietly on with his meal.

Erika's thoughts were spinning, scattering like leaves in a whirlwind. And throughout the meal she found herself giving Noah covert little looks.

With a hand that shook slightly, she took up her glass once more and gazed across at his bent dark head. He'd certainly given her plenty to think about. She stifled a wild laugh. Her body's own quivering response to him had given her plenty to think about for that matter!

Her very innermost thoughts were a confused blur, and she likened her situation to being balanced in the centre of a tightrope. Should she go back to where she'd come from, or should she take a risk and step forward to where everything lay untouched? Brand-new.

'Ah, here comes Rob now.' Noah broke into her thoughts, his words drawing her gaze to where their host was making his way swiftly towards their table.

'He looks a bit upset.' Erika placed her knife and fork neatly together on her plate.

'Problem?' Noah shot the question as Rob pulled up at their table.

'I'm not sure.' The restaurant owner linked them with a rueful glance. 'The fact is I've a young guy who appears to be dead drunk at the bar. Just toppled off his stool.' Rob frowned. 'I don't understand it. He was here last weekend but he was no trouble at all.'

'One of the fruit-pickers?' Noah asked.

'Mmm. Working for old Tony Randazzo.'

Noah snorted. 'Antonio would take a dim view of that kind of behaviour from one of his workers. Like me to check him over?'

'I'd appreciate it.' Rob's mouth tipped. 'I wouldn't want to cost the kid his job. Perhaps if he could sleep it off...'

'How long has he been drinking?' Erika came in quietly, wondering why on earth the staff had continued to serve the young man if he was showing signs of intoxication.

'That's just it.' Rob frowned. 'Apparently he's been here only a short while. He ordered a beer and more or less just keeled over.' He shrugged. 'Must have been hitting something pretty strong earlier. There's a girl with him as well.' His gaze flicked back towards the softly lit cocktail bar. 'She's embarrassed, to say the least. Said it's their first date.'

'I'll come with you, then.' Erika stood swiftly. 'The poor kid must be wondering how she's getting home after this lot.'

Erika's concern deepened, her gaze going from the young man lying in a huddle to the girl pressed up against the wall beside him. 'It's OK,' she reassured her softly. 'We're doctors. We'll look after him. What's your name?'

'Lisa.' The girl's bell of fair hair swung forward across her cheek, her arms winding even more tightly around her midriff. 'He seemed so nice...'

'What's your friend's name, Lisa?' Noah asked, making a swift check on the boy's vital signs.

'James—Jamie Cosgrove. Will he be all right?'

'Let's hope so.' Noah dug out his car keys and handed them over to Rob. 'Could you get my bag, please, mate? Hurry.'

Hearing the urgency in Noah's voice, Erika knelt beside him. 'Found something?' she asked quietly.

He frowned. 'Something doesn't add up here. Check for a bracelet, would you?'

Erika complied, her fingers searching urgently under the young man's long-sleeved shirt. 'Nothing,' she said. 'He's not drunk, is he?'

'No,' Noah growled. 'Catch a whiff of his breath.'

Ketones. Erika's head came up. There was no mistaking the nauseatingly sweet odour. The boy was in a diabetic coma. A sudden movement from behind caught her eye, and she turned and took the bag from Rob. 'Thanks,' she said. 'And will you call an ambulance, please? Tell them we'll need fluids.'

'Then I'll need you to help me get him out the back,' Noah snapped.

Things began happening quickly. Between them the two men got Jamie Cosgrove on to a couch in the small staffroom.

'Thank God you were here.' Rob looked searchingly at Noah. 'What's wrong with him?'

'The lad's obviously a diabetic.' Noah slid open his bag. 'God knows why he's not wearing his Alert bracelet. But don't panic. We can treat him.' His gaze swung to Erika. 'Better take a blood-sugar level. You'll find a glucometer in my bag.'

In a second Erika had what she needed. Her pinprick to the young man's finger was swift, and deftly she scooped the droplet of blood on to the slide. 'It's registering high,' she said, monitoring the glucometer's reading.

'Surprise, surprise,' Noah muttered. 'His BSL must be off the wall. We'll need to take bloods back at the hospital to get an accurate level, but at least we know what we're dealing with. And drunk James is not!'

Two ambulance officers arrived, their presence making the small room seem overcrowded.

Within seconds Erika had the drip going. She caught Noah's eye from the other side of the stretcher. 'I'll go with James in the ambulance. Will you follow?'

'Could I please come?' The earnest little plea left Lisa's mouth in a rush, causing all heads to turn.

Erika's heart went out to her. She looked shattered. 'Are you sure you wouldn't rather go home, Lisa?'

'No.' The girl shook her head. 'James will need someone, won't he?'

Noah's mouth compressed. 'You can come with me,' he said, hitching up his bag and beginning to lead the way outside to his car.

Anne met them at the hospital Casualty entrance. 'And it was shaping up to be a quiet night,' she said ruefully, directing the ambulance officers into a nearby cubicle.

'We'll need to take bloods, Anne.' Erika was already dragging on a white coat. 'And would you set up for an insulin infusion, please?'

'Right.' The charge nurse got busy. 'Do we have a name?'

'James Cosgrove,' Noah said from the doorway. 'I'll give you a hand to get him sorted. Who knows?' He shot a wry look at Erika. 'We may even be able to make it back for our dessert and coffee.'

'Don't bet on it,' Anne warned cheerfully. 'Tara Petani's husband just brought her in.'

'She's definitely in labour?' Erika knuckled a hand to her forehead.

'Oh, yes.' Anne sent them a dry smile. 'She's been packing apples all day. Thought it was just backache as a result.'

Noah looked torn.

'Go.' Erika sensed his dilemma. 'Look after Tara. I'll stay with Jamie.'

'So much for your time off,' Noah muttered as he left them.

'This place needs two permanent doctors,' Anne lamented. 'Already Noah's chasing his tail, and he's not even officially back from leave.'

Erika chewed the inside of her cheek, looking thoughtful as she unclipped her pen and began to write on Jamie's chart.

'That's it, Jamie... He's coming round,' Anne said a few minutes later.

'Good.' Erika looked up from the chart. 'I've ordered his blood sugar levels to be checked every fifteen minutes for the next hour, Anne.'

'I'll pass it on at hand-over. I'm off duty soon.' Her skilled fingers reached for her young patient's wrist. 'Improving,' she smiled.

The boy's eyes opened.

'Jamie?' Erika said softly. 'I'm Dr Somers. You collapsed at the restaurant.'

'Where am I?' he croaked, and licked his lips.

'In hospital. You're doing fine,' Erika told him, but thought that was stretching it. His clamminess had receded and he had more colour, but he still looked grotty. 'We'll need to have a chat, but that can wait. In the meantime, I want you to rest. OK?'

James's even white teeth clipped his lower lip. 'H-how long will I be here?'

Erika did a mental rundown of his treatment. He'd need the drip for possibly two days, and it would be prudent to keep him under observation for at least one more day after that. 'About three days, if all goes well. Lisa's outside,' she added with a smile.

'She must think I'm a real jerk.' James turned his face to the wall.

'She's very concerned about you, actually.' Erika placed a hand on his shoulder. 'What about a quick visit before we settle you for the night?'

The boy's eyes flickered open and then closed. 'Yeah—OK...'

Later, on her way back to the station, Erika stopped outside Jamie's cubicle and peeped in, smiling at what she saw. Lisa's fair head was bent to him and she was clasping his hand.

Young love, she mused, rubbing wearily at the back of her neck. Good luck to them.

'Fancy a cup of tea?' Anne fell into step beside her.

'Love one. I'll make it,' Erika offered.

'Thanks. I'll hand over and be with you in a tick.'

Erika stepped into the kitchen, inhaling the faint aroma of spices. She smiled wryly. Bev Patten's stamp of ownership lay everywhere. As the hospital's chef, her dedication to the nutritional welfare of both patients and staff was total.

After plugging the electric kettle in, Erika crossed to the window and stood looking out. The darkness of night was now complete, interspersed with only a few tiny lights twinkling around the township.

She touched the fine gold chain at her throat, sighing for something she couldn't put a name to. As for her evening with Noah? Well, she certainly hadn't expected it to end like this...

'Well, that's the end of my late shifts for another month!' Anne came lightly into the kitchen, slinging her shoulder bag across the back of a chair.

'Who looks after Holly when you're on lates?' Erika asked. Anne had already mentioned all her family lived miles away in the city.

'I've a terrific neighbour,' Anne smiled. 'Jacqui Mitchell. Holly sleeps over and it works out quite well. Jacqui has her own son, Isaac. He's eight. Very gentle with Holly, though. Oh, not those,' she said, seeing Erika take a couple of teabags from the box. 'Let's make a pot of tea. And toast. Bev should have a bit of bread somewhere. Lord, I'm famished!'

Erika looked on in amusement, collecting several digestive biscuits for her own consumption.

'So, how was your dinner with Noah?' Anne settled herself beside the toaster and looked up expectantly.

Erika paused in the act of pouring boiling water into the teapot. 'Fine,' she said throatily. 'The food was lovely. And the atmosphere...'

Anne chuckled. 'That's not quite what I asked.'

'No.' Erika's heart revved up a notch, and she became aware of a faint air of expectancy running between them. Oh, what the heck! If she voiced her intentions to Anne, it might put some credibility into the whole situation. 'I—may be staying on after my locum tenure finishes. At least, Noah's asked me to consider it.'

'Alleluia!' Anne began spreading butter on her toast. 'He's been desperate to get another MO for the practice.' She chuckled, licking a scattering of crumbs from her fingers. 'I'd go so far as to say he was preparing himself to do just about anything.'

Like what? Erika was suddenly off balance, a sick hollow in her stomach as she recalled his praise. And how in just a few hours he'd made her feel almost indispensable. And then, very sure of himself, he'd settled it with a kiss.

Erika felt goosebumps break out all over her. She'd been set up so beautifully. She was even beginning to doubt now his supposedly coincidental early arrival back today...

'It's common knowledge he borrowed heavily to get the practice up and running,' Anne said, inadvertently adding more fuel to Erika's apprehension. 'It would be a disaster if he had to pack it in. We've all been living in dread he'd do just that if he got stretched beyond his limits again. But if you're going to stay...?' The nurse smiled ingenuously.

Erika swallowed an angry retort. 'I haven't made any decision yet, Anne. Far from it!'

'Oh—I thought— No, I didn't think.' The

nurse's voice was strained. 'I shouldn't have run off at the mouth. Oh, hell,' she sighed. 'Let's talk about something else.'

'You'll get no argument from me on that.' Erika looked down at the milky tea in her mug and thought the whole scenario might have had a lighter side if she didn't feel so hurt. And she'd been such an easy target. Vulnerable. Wanting to make her own decisions without her father pulling strings. Wanting to do the best job for Noah. In a strange way wanting to belong...

'Did Dirk go with you on the descent this afternoon?'

Erika shook her head. 'He mentioned being shorthanded. Said he was needed to co-ordinate the air-lift.'

'I'll bet that miffed him.' Anne's laugh had a slight edge.

'In what way?' Erika blinked, made herself focus. She felt suddenly out of kilter. Exhausted, as though she'd just run a marathon.

'Oh, Dirk just loves dicing with danger and destiny!' Anne spread her small hand across the table, clenching it. 'I don't know how he can expect me to live with that kind of uncertainty again.'

Erika's mind keyed in caution. Had she missed something here? Was there a relationship between Anne and Dirk Belzar? 'I got the impression Dirk was very competent. I can't see him taking unnecessary risks.'

Anne grimaced. 'He maintains it's a privilege to

be chosen to carry out emergency retrieval work. But he's a brilliant phys ed teacher, with a wonderful influence on the kids. Why can't he be satisfied with that?'

Erika spread her hands in defeat and stood to her feet, collecting their tea things. If they were talking about risky undertakings, nursing these days was hardly a doddle. But obviously Anne was in no mood to admit that.

Sighing inwardly, Erika ran water into the sink, shot in detergent and churned the water into suds.

'Ah—ladies.' Noah appeared in the doorway. With a lift of his brows he stared at Erika, almost elbow-deep in foam. 'A spot of domesticity, Dr Somers? Very nice.'

Erika sent him a flinty look. 'Makes a change from wallowing in Hibiclens.' A bolt of residual anger had her dunking the mugs and glaring into the detergent bubbles.

'Cup of tea, Noah?' Anne blocked a yawn and investigated the teapot. 'Oh—I'll have to make fresh.'

'Not on my account, Annie. Why don't you get off home?'

'Mmm. Think I will.' She hitched up her bag. 'Night, you two.'

'Night,' they echoed.

'Like a hand?'

Erika felt Noah's touch on her shoulder and turned her head. 'You could make yourself useful and wipe up.'

'OK.' He seemed unfazed, plucking a crisp teatowel off the rack and making short work of the few items. 'You should've shoved it all in the dishwasher,' he reproved lightly.

Erika made a small moue of distaste. 'I didn't feel like taking liberties in Bev's domain.'

'Cautious little thing, aren't you?'

Erika snorted inwardly. Obviously not nearly cautious enough where he was concerned. She began to fuss round unnecessarily. Why was he prowling about in here? she fretted. And what about his patient? She gave a final swipe to the benchtop. 'How's Tara doing?'

Soft humour gleamed briefly in his eyes. 'Well occupied for the next little while. I've time to drive you home. You can fill me in about James on the way.'

'You don't have to trouble.' Hastily she rearranged the teatowel on its rack. 'I can arrange for a taxi.'

Noah's eyes narrowed. 'What's wrong, Erika?'

'Nothing.'

'Everything,' he refuted. 'You're grumpy and out of sync.' Placing his hands on her shoulders, he turned her gently towards him.

'It's been a long day.' Erika set her mouth, determinedly telling herself she wasn't feeling what she was faintly ashamed of feeling. That his closeness wasn't making her almost sick with nerves. Vulnerable all over again. Exposed. She licked her lips and tried to ease her shoulders. Automatically, they tightened again.

'I'm sorry our evening had to end the way it did.' The huskiness in his voice ran all over her bones. She could hardly drag air into her lungs.

'What exactly do you want from me, Noah?' Her voice contained a thread of bitterness.

His look sharpened, and then he grinned. A sexy, puckish grin that had her heart somersaulting. 'Cup of coffee when we get to your place?'

CHAPTER FIVE

'So, HOW is James doing?' Noah posed the question as the car slid out of a dense pocket of fog and into the clear once more.

'He seems to have picked up fairly well.' Erika leaned into the soft leather behind her and ordered her mind to focus. 'I'll talk to him tomorrow—'

'I'll talk to him,' Noah interposed firmly. 'You're off duty.'

She gave a brittle sigh. 'I've told him we'll need to keep him for possibly three days. I'd be grateful if you'd stick to that. I want him to have some re-education about his diabetes. It's obvious he's become a bit slack.'

'We have reams of stuff he can read,' Noah confirmed. 'Or a video cassette if that's easier for him to absorb.' He laughed drily. 'Perhaps little Lisa might give him the impetus to get his act together.'

'And perhaps "little Lisa" is the very reason he got distracted in the first place and didn't up his insulin when he should have.'

'Too much fruit?'

'I'd say so. And if it's his first time picking, and I have the impression it is, he's literally pigged out—not realising it would dramatically alter the level of his blood sugar.'

'And the absence of his Alert bracelet?' Noah slowed the vehicle as they turned into her street.

Erika chewed her lip. 'Nervous about this date with Lisa. Left it off deliberately. Didn't want to have to explain. Appear as a lame duck.'

'Or drake.' Noah gave her a teasing grin, which she pointedly didn't return, and came to a stop in the driveway.

'What's your version, then, Doctor?' Releasing her seatbelt, Erika edged into the corner of the seat.

'Same as yours.' Noah leaned towards her. 'Well done.'

Erika stiffened, the faint, elusive scent of his cologne catching her nostrils, and something snapped inside her. 'Why don't you just give up, Noah?'

'Sorry?'

'Apportioning these great dollops of approval!' she ground out, pitching out of the Land Rover, almost twisting her ankle in the process.

In her agitation she dropped her keys on the porch and Noah, right behind her, picked them up. Refusing to do anything so undignified as trying to wrestle them from him, she stood back and allowed him to open the door.

There was puzzlement on Noah's face as he followed her inside.

'Will instant do?' she asked tersely, dropping her jacket and clutch bag on to a handy chair. 'The coffee maker's on the blink.'

'Since when?' Noah followed her into the kitchen.

'I don't remember.' She shovelled both hands through her hair. 'A couple of days. And before you ask, no, I haven't taken it to be fixed.'

'When are you going to start looking after yourself, Erika?' He eased her aside and filled the kettle. 'You skip meals, run yourself ragged over the patients, sit toiling in the surgery when you should be long gone.'

'Who told you that?' she said tiredly. 'Your spies?'

'My what?' His eyebrows shot up.

'Cut the innocent act, Noah.' Erika kicked off her high heels, then immediately wished she hadn't. She'd suddenly lost several centimetres and most of her poise. 'Anyway.' She turned away, her face half hidden in shadow. 'You won't have to worry about me for much longer. I'll be gone.'

'When did you decide all this?' he demanded. 'And why?'

Why? He had a nerve! A surge of anger coupled with a sharp disappointment rose in Erika. 'I'm not about to let myself be used, Doctor.'

'Used?' Noah's face was still.

She shrugged carelessly. 'Well, if I'm here on a permanent basis, it will generate more income, won't it? Enough to pay off your mortgage quite nicely.'

'What the hell are you on about?' The words were curt, forced out.

Her little snort had a hollow ring. 'Oh, I've heard a few things tonight. How you're up to your eyebrows in debt. You even admitted as much to me yourself.' She swallowed convulsively. 'Any half-decent locum would have done. As long as the applicant was female—'

'Now, just a minute!' He met her eyes, his reflecting anger. 'Are you accusing me of using sexual persuasion to get you to stay on and practise here?'

'If the cap fits...' Erika was past considering what she was saying.

'I've never heard such rot!' Noah snapped forward and took her by the shoulders. 'And where's your own self-worth in all this, Dr Somers?' he mocked. 'You have to know you have skills above the average. Why wouldn't I consider myself damned lucky to have you as a locum? And why wouldn't I try to hang on to you, if you wanted to stay? What's sinister about that?'

Put like that, nothing. Nothing at all. Erika's head dipped forward and she felt the tight lens of tears across her eyes. What he'd said made a nonsense of her suspicions. She cringed inwardly at her wild accusations. She must be losing her grip, or be plain overtired. 'Noah...' She swallowed the lump in her throat. 'If I've misjudged you—'

'*If!*' He shook his head as if to clear it. 'All right, let's get it all out in the open.'

'You don't have to explain.' Erika pressed her hands together, her expression suddenly pinched.

'Oh, but I do,' he said, his voice polite and impersonal. 'And the hospital grapevine is correct. I do have a considerable mortgage, but by working my tail off I've always been able to service it.' He turned from her, throwing his arms wide. 'Coming here, getting the practice established, was something I always wanted to do. And I did it for a reason. At the time I was engaged to be married.'

The whistle on the kettle shrilled, but neither of them paid it any heed.

Erika continued to look at him with pain-filled eyes. She just knew what he was about to tell her.

'Justine and I met when we were both relative newcomers to general practice. We'd both got jobs at one of those satellite suburban practices that are springing up all over the place now. To cut a long story short, we clicked. Decided we had a future together, personally and professionally. After our contracts expired, she went overseas to gain some experience in internal medicine. I set out to find a suitable practice to buy. At that stage we both wanted something in the country. Somewhere to raise kids...'

The four words echoed bitterly around them. Erika took a ragged breath. 'So—you came to Hillcrest?'

'Yes.' He rubbed a hand through his hair. 'It was rundown. The practice, I mean. But there seemed huge potential.' He sent her a wry look. 'And most of all the people wanted me—us,' he corrected. 'I finally got the bank's approval to re-site the surgery to where it is now, build a modest house.' He laughed without humour. 'I needn't have bothered with the house. When Justine finally joined me, she stayed only a few weeks. Decided Hillcrest wasn't her style—or, more to the point, *I* wasn't her style. She left and I was on my own, trying to serve a practice that should have had two doctors in the first place…'

Erika shook her head, her eyes full of compassion. 'Oh, Noah…'

His mouth twisted wryly. 'Is that all you can say, Dr Somers?'

She looked dismayed for a moment. 'I jumped to all the wrong conclusions, didn't I?'

'You did,' he agreed softly, drawing her to him, stroking his thumbs along her jaw, searching her eyes, as if to peel away her innermost thoughts layer by layer.

Erika licked her lips, her normal thought patterns jamming as he gently turned her face up towards him.

'Erika…' he sighed huskily, his mouth locking against hers, his hands skimming the soft straps of her camisole from her shoulders, smoothing her skin.

Noah. Somewhere in her head she said his name, and then kissed him back, their need blazingly mutual, a fierce, overwhelming hunger.

Lifting her hands, she buried them in the springy darkness of his hair, letting the strands flutter past her fingers, cradling him closer and closer.

'You're perfect.' He seemed entranced, his

mouth sipping along her jaw, her throat, the deep hollow between her breasts. 'So perfect...'

The intrusive tattoo of his bleep had them reeling back to sharp reality. Erika crossed her arms, unobtrusively righting her straps. 'Hospital?'

'Afraid so.' Noah blew out a fractured breath as he returned the electronic messenger to his pocket.

'Oh—your coffee!'

'No time.' His lips folded in on a smile. 'Tara wants to start pushing.' Lifting his hands, he trailed his fingers across her flushed cheeks, a faint questioning in their exploration. 'You make it very hard to leave,' he said quietly.

What do you think you're doing? Erika stared into the bathroom mirror, as if demanding an answer from her wide-eyed reflection. It was very clear to her she'd opened to Noah Jameson in a way she'd never done with any man. Had she left herself even more vulnerable?

For a long time she'd been content to let her life jog along, to let the future take care of itself. But now... With Noah...

CHAPTER SIX

Erika woke to the sun striping a rainbow across the end of her bed and the muffled ringing of the front doorbell.

'All right, all right!' she muttered, feeling around for something to cover her T-shirt nightie.

'Yes—what is it?' She flung open the door. 'Noah...' she stated softly, and in some surprise.

'Caught you napping, did I?' He gave a mocking lift to his eyebrows, his gaze homing in on her hand clutching the edges of her thin cotton robe.

'What time is it?' Flushing slightly, she stood back to let him in.

'Eight o'clock. And it's a beautiful day.'

Erika made a non-committal moue and closed the door. 'Something I can do for you?' Unselfconsciously she blocked a yawn, and riffled a hand through her hair.

He chuckled. 'You're the doctor—you tell me.'

Her head whipped up. His eyes held a direct challenge. And their shared kisses last night came back in searing detail. She swallowed, her breathing suddenly erratic.

'I've come to invite you to a game of tennis.' He sauntered towards the window, turning abruptly to spread his hands across the back of the lounge chair.

Tennis? She blinked uncertainly. Her senses were in total disarray, having this big sexy man here so early in the morning in the quiet intimacy of her flat. She swallowed against the peculiar dryness in her mouth. He was dressed in white rugger shorts and a navy polo shirt, looking so fresh, so fit, so—so everything!

'It's my day off, Noah,' she pointed out, desperate to take both her mind and his off the subject of their mutual attraction.

'I know.' He grinned. 'But some exercise will benefit us both, Erika.'

'I got enough exercise yesterday, climbing down that cliff, thank you,' she refused darkly. 'And what makes you think I can play tennis anyway?'

'A little bird told me.'

Erika clicked her tongue and then remembered. She'd made up a foursome with Jenny's social tennis club one day last week.

She stared aggrievedly at him. 'Do you know everything about me?'

Laughing, he shook his head. 'But I'm getting there. You don't seem much of a morning person.' With a quick twist of his muscular body, he dodged the cushion she threw at him.

Giving release to a reluctant chuckle, Erika went through to the bedroom. In two seconds her head came back round the door. 'What did Tara have?'

'A little boy.' Noah's eyes softened. 'Perfect six-and-a-half-pounder.'

'Tara OK?'

'She's very well. I've already been in to see her this morning. And I dare say she's making better use of her time than we seem to be.' Leaning back against the window, he folded his arms across his chest. 'Get a move on, Dr Somers. We only have the court until eleven.'

She sent him a wide-eyed, innocent look. 'I don't have a racquet with me.'

'I have two.'

She sighed. Of course he had two. She had a quick wash and cleaned her teeth, wondering if she had anything fit to wear.

A quick rifle through her clothes brought forth a pair of white shorts and a nautical-looking blue and white striped T-shirt. Lord, they'd look almost like twins!

Huffing a hollow laugh, she knotted a bright red pullover around her middle. Then, bending low, she caught up her long sweep of hair, securing it on top of her head with a giant-sized butterfly clip.

'What court are we using?' Erika looked across at Noah as he nosed the Land Rover out of her street.

'The one at the school.'

'Do you play often?'

'Tennis?'

'Very droll,' she said mildly. 'I meant are you in a fixture round or anything?'

'I'd like to be, but the nature of medicine, especially in this set-up, makes it nigh impossible to be available at any given time. What about you?' He sent her an under-brow look as he changed gears. 'Do you play?'

'Mmm. Sometimes.' Erika looked thoughtful. 'We have a court at home.'

Within a few minutes they were at their destination, Noah coasting to a stop beside the tree-lined fence of the schoolyard. 'OK, Dr Somers,' he said. 'Let's see what you're made of.' Cutting the engine, he swung out into the crisp morning air.

Am I supposed to be intimidated? Erika wondered, watching him execute a few callisthenic exercises, some running on the spot, deep breathing. More like impressed, she decided, her mouth curving into a wry little smile. Turning her back on him, she began her own warm-up of a few stretches against the steel-framed fence.

'Ready?' She shot him a sweetly innocent smile, taking the racquet he handed her and walking smartly across to the enclosed tennis court.

Shrugging off the loss of the first two games, Erika consoled herself that she was just getting her eye in. But Noah was good, she recognised. Strong and purposeful.

At the other end of the court, Noah alternated his feet rhythmically on the spot and watched for Erika's first service. He could tell already she was a precise player, fast and accurate. And those legs!

Poetry in motion! Concentrate, Jameson, he derided. This lady is no push-over.

Taking a moment to gather herself, Erika rocketed her first service in, the ball kicking up the chalk as it ripped past Noah. Just out. He raised his racquet in acknowledgement, narrowing his eyes in concentration.

Game after game they tested one another, both sweating with exertion, the score see-sawing until Erika had the advantage, the longed-for chance of clenching the game and set.

Pulling back, she struck the ball, a low grunt of satisfaction accompanying its speeding passage straight past him.

Bemusedly he watched the ball's trajectory and shook his head. 'You aced me!'

Slightly breathless, laughing, Erika ran up to the net. 'Game and set to me, I think. Shake.'

'Hey, we agreed two sets.' Noah enclosed her smaller hand in his. 'Don't I get the chance to break even?'

'Not today.' She puffed the tiny tendrils of hair off her forehead. 'My legs won't go another minute. We'll have to make time for a re-match.'

'You'd better believe it,' he growled, marching her off the court to the rough-hewn benches outside.

'You're not a sore loser, are you, Dr Jameson?'

He gave a rueful little smile. 'Just a tad humiliated.' He dug through his sports bag and produced several bottles of chilled water.

'Thanks.' Erika accepted one gratefully.

'So, Erika Somers.' A rather dry smile tugged his mouth. 'Were you stringing me along?'

Tilting her head to one side, laughter reined in, she answered softly, 'Going back a few years, runner-up in the Victorian junior hardcourt titles.'

Noah whistled through his teeth. 'I guess I should be thankful I lost by only one point.'

Wrinkling her nose at him, Erika settled back against the wire-mesh fence, letting her gaze drift over the soft green of the trees, the distant bony ridge of mountains...

'Why the big sigh?'

Erika lifted a shoulder. 'Just thinking.'

'Are you going to tell me?'

She tipped her head back. A light mist was clearing, leaving patches of intensely blue sky. If only she could stop the world right here, she thought fancifully. 'I guess I have some decisions to make, don't I?'

'Only if you want to.' Noah was looking expectantly at her. 'I don't want to pressure you.'

'I know that now.' She huffed a jagged laugh. 'I'm sorry I went off the deep end at you last night.'

'Forgotten already.' He raised a hand, trickling his knuckles over her cheek. 'Care to tell me why you're so far away from home, Erika?'

She spun her head down, twisting the bottle of water between her palms, remaining silent.

'Does it all revolve around your family?' he pressed gently.

'Probably.' Her shoulders drooped. 'Oh, don't get me wrong...I love them all to bits. But sometimes my dad—well, he comes on rather strongly.'

'He has a lot of clout, Erika. Ewen Somers is hardly unknown in Australian medical circles.'

'Don't I know it!' She gave a tight laugh. 'It's just very hard to gauge your real self-worth when your father is so well known, and not averse to pulling strings on your behalf.'

'He obviously wanted to give you a soft ride through medicine.'

'Cushion-soft,' she snorted.

'And it wouldn't have been what you wanted at all,' he observed astutely, holding her brown eyes with his own brilliant blue gaze.

'I think he was disappointed when my two older brothers chose law instead of following him into medicine. And when I eventually showed an interest in doing medicine he was so proud...' She stopped and licked her lips. 'For the most part I've managed to be my own person, but Dad's always been in the background offering to "sort something out"—which usually meant calling in a favour from one of his specialist colleagues.'

Noah slanted a measured look at her, imagining her independent nature would have revolted at that kind of blatant nepotism.

She took a mouthful of water before continuing softly. 'When I came back from overseas, Dad had more or less convinced himself and everybody else I was going to specialise, like him.'

'But you had other ideas?'

She nodded. 'I went and did my GP training. But even that didn't stop him from trying to organise my life. When I'd completed my contract, he told me he'd had a word with one of his buddies and there was a place for me in a very up-market suburban practice. Regular surgery hours, time off. Even a service that covered the night-calls.' She grimaced. 'He nearly flipped when I told him I was coming here to Hillcrest to do a locum.'

A little frown reached Noah's eyes. 'In a way, did you come here to spite him?'

'Of course not!' She looked offended. 'I came because I wanted to make use of my training and in the process do a good job. And I needed the advantage of distance to get my head together about my personal life.' She swallowed. 'I'll be thirty-one next birthday.'

'I'll be thirty-five.' Noah looked at her gravely. 'Staggering towards imminent aged-care, aren't we?' He drained the last of his water and threw the empty bottle into a nearby receptacle. 'And this chap Alistair; where does he fit in?'

She took a deep breath, stunned to think she'd hardly thought of Alistair at all lately. 'That's what I have to decide.'

'So stay on here until the answer presents itself,' Noah said practically.

Could it be that easy? Erika made a face at him.

'You just want a chance to beat me at tennis.' She felt suddenly light-hearted, as though merely talking to Noah about it had more than halved her problem. 'OK if I let you know tomorrow?'

'Sure.' Suddenly he turned his head up, listening. 'Hear that?'

'What?' Erika frowned, and then heard the sound too—the high-pitched roar of a motorcycle coming closer and travelling much too fast. 'Heavens!' Her eyes flew wide. 'He's coming this way!'

'Crazy fool!' Noah leapt to his feet, taking her with him. 'He'll never make that corner!' Shoving Erika back against the wire netting, he shielded her with his body as the biker hurtled wildly past.

Within seconds he was skidding out of control, striking a pothole in the road. The force sent him skywards before he landed under the sickening thump of metal.

'Get my bag!' Noah was off and running towards the mangled heap of bike and victim.

Erika moved like lightning. Throwing herself into the driver's seat of the Land Rover, she used the car phone to call the ambulance. Then, hefting Noah's medical bag from its space, she tumbled back out of the vehicle and sprinted towards the accident scene.

Noah had the heavy bike almost lifted off the crumpled body. 'One more should do it.' He breathed harshly, his muscles straining as he braced the partially raised bike against his legs and heaved it upright.

Simultaneously they snapped on gloves and dropped to the injured youth's side.

'How bad is it?' Erika felt her mouth dry. The boy was not even wearing proper leathers.

'I'll know in a minute.' Noah's hands moved with swift sureness over their patient's body. 'Ambulance on its way?'

'Yes.' Erika nodded. 'Pete Delgado's on duty. I've told him to bring haemacell.'

'Looks like we'll need it.' Noah's mouth compressed. 'Possible severed femoral artery, by the look of it. Tourniquet, please, Erika. Quick!'

Erika's hands were steady as she handed over the belt-like elastic band and then bent to monitor the youth's vital signs.

'Pulse?' Noah rapped, securing the tourniquet around the boy's upper thigh.

'Rapid and thready. He's not responding to stimuli. Pupils dilated. I'll get an IV in.' Seconds later she said tensely, 'I can't find a vein.'

Noah's head jerked up. 'This is a bloody nightmare... And where the hell is Pete?'

'OK, I've got it. IV's in and holding.' Erika's words came out in a rush of relief.

Noah swore, his brow furrowing in concentration. 'BP's dropping like a stone. Come on!' he breathed to the boy's unconscious form. 'Don't shut down on me.'

At last the ambulance siren could be heard.

Pete Delgado screamed to a halt beside them,

delivering the flask of haemacell to Erika's outstretched hands. She passed it across to Noah.

'Thanks.' He looked up briefly. 'We'll run it stat, and pin our hopes on it keeping him stable until he gets some blood.'

'Think he'll make it, Doc?' Pete hunkered down, his look solemn.

'Let's be positive.' Noah secured the IV line. 'We'll race straight over to Warwick, Pete. He needs to be in the care of a surgeon. Call through, would you? Let them know our ETA and that we'll need a blood specimen and cross-match immediately on arrival.'

'I found some ID in his saddlebag.' Erika flipped open the leather wallet. 'Damon Clewes and a Warwick address.'

'Give it to the police when they get here,' Noah said grimly. 'It'll be up to them to get hold of the family. But at least we'll be able to give the hospital a name.'

Damon was stretchered gently into the ambulance.

'I'll go with him.' Noah put out a hand and touched Erika's wrist. 'Your guess is as good as mine when I'll be back.'

She nodded. 'Good luck. I'll leave your Land Rover at the hospital and the keys at the nurses' station.'

'Thanks.' The lines of strain etched deeper around his mouth. 'I'll be in touch,' he called, before swinging the doors of the ambulance firmly shut.

Erika stood quite still until the last of the siren's echoes had died away. Now that the adrenalin high of the past few minutes had receded, she felt oddly disorientated, as though it had all happened to someone else.

Sighing, she made her way back along the dusty strip to the Land Rover to wait for the police. It would be a relief to hand everything over to them. Casting a quick look behind her at the mangled bike, she gave a shudder.

It was early afternoon before Erika got back to the hospital. She realised she was starving, and went along to the kitchen to find something to eat. Later, refreshed by several cups of tea and a salad sandwich, she decided to put a bit of zip into her afternoon and pop in on Tara and her baby.

Erika put on a smile as she tapped on Tara's door and popped her head in. 'Hi, there! How's the new mum?'

'Oh, Dr Somers—Erika.' Tara's eyes lit up. 'Come on in.'

'Definitely an informal visit,' Erika promised. 'See—no white coat and no stethoscope. Would you believe I've been playing tennis?'

'You look fabulous.' Tara was sitting up in bed nursing her son. 'I, on the other hand,' she grumbled mildly, 'feel like an empty sack of potatoes.'

Erika husked a low laugh. 'That'll pass. How's

the bub?' Perching on the edge of the bed, she skated a finger over the infant's downy head.

'Gorgeous.' Tara's eyes shone. 'As you can see, I'm a bit prejudiced.'

'And with good reason, I'd say. How did Michael cope?' Erika knew Tara's young husband had been nervous about attending the birth of his child.

'Magnificently. Surprised the socks off me.' The new mother beamed mistily. 'Noah even let him cut the cord.'

'That's brilliant.' Erika's look was soft. And how lovely of Noah to have let that happen, she thought, feeling a little dip in her stomach. An ache she couldn't quite explain.

'And your labour, Tara?' Moving off the bed, Erika fetched a chair to sit on. 'Was it OK?'

Tara made a small face. 'Panic stations when I knew the baby was actually coming. But everyone here at the hospital was great—Noah especially. Still, I'm relieved he wasn't huge,' she confided, holding her son more tightly.

'Have you decided on a name for this new little man?' Erika asked with a smile.

'Jacob,' Tara said without hesitation.

Erika put out a hand, stroking the tightly clenched tiny fist. 'That's a good strong name,' she approved. 'Probably get shortened to Jake when he goes to school, though.'

'Or before,' Tara agreed with a philosophical grin. 'Do you know anything about infant massage?' she asked after a minute. 'I've been reading a bit about it. How it's supposed to be good for their digestion.'

'Helps their circulation too.' Erika nodded. 'Nice way for you to bond as well.' She smiled. 'I'll show you the technique before you leave hospital, if you like?'

'Oh, could you? That'd be great. How much time does it take?' Tara's dark eyes were thoughtful. 'It's just that until we can afford some help I'll still have to give Michael a hand with the farm work.'

'Ten minutes is ample for a newborn.' Her gaze soft, Erika watched Tara ease her son from her breast and kiss the top of his head. She swallowed. 'May I?' she asked gently, holding her arms out for the baby.

'We're so lucky to have you here in Hillcrest,' Tara said earnestly. 'You and Noah.' Tenting her knees under the sheet, she linked her arms around them. 'You're both really tuned in.'

'Nice of you to say so.' Carefully Erika placed the infant back in his crib, her eyes wistful as she looked down at his breathtaking perfection. 'Medicine's become more patient-friendly these days, that's all.'

'There's a whisper going about you may be staying on...?' Tara's dark eyes widened in query.

'I haven't quite decided yet.' Which wasn't exactly the truth, Erika derided silently, a wild kind of expectancy hurtling through her veins. But there was no way she could leave without testing the strength of these feelings for Noah. And, more to the point, to see if they were reciprocated. 'Pretty flowers,' she deflected quickly, touching her fingers to the creamy petals in their pottery vase.

'My early freesias.' Tara blocked a yawn. 'Michael brought them in first thing this morning. I think he pulled them up bulbs and all.'

Erika chuckled. 'It's the thought that counts. Get some rest now,' she advised. 'Don't forget you're a brand-new mum. I'll see you tomorrow.'

CHAPTER SEVEN

JUST before midday the next day, Erika made her way slowly up the stairs to the surgery, her leg muscles protesting every inch of the way.

She made a small face. She'd over-exercised yesterday; that was evident. All the more reason to get back into a daily pattern of keeping fit, she resolved.

'You're early.' Jenny greeted her with a wide smile. 'Nice weekend?'

Erika grinned wryly. 'It was until I played tennis with Noah yesterday. My muscles are screaming.' Taking the few steps behind Reception, she plonked on to a high stool.

'You saw quite a bit of each other, then?' Jenny's green look was rife with curiosity.

'Quite a bit.' Erika lifted a shoulder, pulling the desk diary towards her, shaking her head in rueful conjecture. Would she ever get used to small-town gossip? How the way news, good and bad, was telegraphed almost before it happened? Yet there was no sense of maliciousness in it, she owned. Just a small community working together. Surviving together.

'My niece works as a waitress at Peaches.'

Jenny eyed her keenly. 'She said you looked gorgeous.'

Erika looked up innocently. 'Just something I threw on.'

The secretary looked taken aback. 'You always look lovely,' she said generously, turning aside to answer the ringing phone.

'Hello, Erika.'

Noah. Her mouth dried as she swung round. He was standing against the doorframe, big and handsome, dressed in casual chinos and a collarless pinstriped shirt. 'Morning—or is it afternoon?' She hiccuped a laugh.

'Just on, I think.' He glanced at his watch.

Jenny's brows rose. 'Ready for the off?' Clipping the receiver back into place, she took the mail he handed her.

'Not quite. Couple of referrals there, Jen. I'd like them away today, please. I've asked for appointments asap. The secretaries will no doubt get back to us with the details.' He lifted his head and stared straight at Erika. 'Come on through.'

'Sure.' Erika slid off the stool, her heart lurching into a mad scattering of beats as she followed him into his consulting room.

'Sorry I didn't get back to you yesterday.' Noah spun out a chair and placed it next to his own. 'I didn't get back from Warwick until late afternoon.' He rubbed at the back of his neck. 'You'll be pleased to know our lad is stable and he'll keep his leg.'

Erika smiled. 'So our emergency treatment worked. Well done, doctor.'

'Hey, you were there too, don't forget.'

'But you were the one the onus fell on. I always think that lonely ride in the ambulance with a seriously ill patient is nightmare material.'

His laugh was a bit hollow. 'Well, it kind of comes with the territory, doesn't it?' He fixed her with a meaningful gaze. She had such beautiful brown eyes he almost forgot what he wanted to say. 'What did you do with yourself, then?'

'Laundry mostly.' Erika gave a cracked laugh, sliding her fingers underneath the unbuttoned collar of her shirt. 'I did have a nice visit with Tara, though.'

He gave a huff of laughter and spun his gaze to the ceiling. It wasn't the reaction she'd expected. 'I—made a decision too,' she said quietly. 'About the future.'

'And?'

She bit her lip, watching as his broad chest rose and fell in a shaken sigh. 'I'm staying—Noah!' She gave a muted shriek as he pulled her upright. 'What are you doing!'

'Just this.' Laughing softly, he whirled her in a circle, then gathered her in, his eyes on her face with the intensity of a camera lens. 'We'll be good together,' he said with conviction.

She nodded weakly. 'I hope so.'

'I know so,' he murmured, bending to kiss her mouth, taking his time over it, until she parted her lips, drinking him in, feeling the absorption of his scent in her nostrils, through her skin. The scent of a man. Her man?

When they drew apart, they stared at one another, the moment almost surreal. While outside the circle of their fantasy the world went on. Birds called to each other, the faint hum of a farm tractor rose and fell in the distance, a telephone rang and was silenced.

Noah was the first to break the stillness with a tattered sigh. 'I feel as though I've been kicked by a mule.'

'Make that two.' Erika rested her head against his chest, feeling the solid thud of his heart. Never in her wildest dreams had she imagined being with a man who could make her feel like this—so powerful, in a way, so giving. A long breath jagged its way from her lungs. 'Come on,' she rallied. 'Let's get the wheels back on this practice. You're supposed to be handing over to me.'

He touched her hair, his hand lingering over its deep auburn silkiness. 'I wish now I hadn't planned to go any-damned-where this week.'

She drew in a breath, a wave of reaction causing her to clench her fingers. If the truth be known, she didn't want him going anywhere either. But, on the other hand, she desperately needed time to sort herself out, away from his compelling influence. And there was Alistair as well...

'Just where are you spending the rest of your leave?'

'I'm flying to Brisbane this afternoon to see my folks. Have to catch up with the newest member of the Jameson clan as well.' Keeping his hand on her nape, he settled her back into her chair. 'My brother, Paul, and his wife, Kim, have recently become the proud parents of a son.'

'Oh—that's nice.' Again Erika felt that odd little ache deep within her. 'What did they call him?'

'Steven—after Dad. They have a four-year-old daughter as well, Dakota.'

Erika's eyebrows rose. 'Unusual name.'

'She's an enchanting child,' he said proudly.

'And you're a doting uncle by the sound of it.' She gazed up at him, her chin cupped in her hand. 'I'll bet you've bought her a present as well?'

He nodded, his grin faintly sheepish. 'Last week when I was in Sydney. I got her some fairy stuff. That's still the go, isn't it?'

She huffed a laugh. 'For little girls, fairy stuff is always the go. Is Paul your only sibling?'

'Mmm.' He picked up her hand and ran his fingers across her knuckles. 'What about your family? Are either of your brothers married?'

'Dean is. Jacinta, his wife, is a lawyer too. Well, they're barristers really.'

'Any children?'

'No.' She sent him a dry look. 'I don't know when they'd find the time. I'm sure my parents would love grandchildren. Most of their friends have several by now.'

He squeezed the tips of her fingers. 'Perhaps it'll be down to you,' he said softly.

The thought brought a faint heat to her skin. Her heart gave a strange little flutter and she tried not to notice how the soft fabric of his chinos moulded his thigh. And how that translated into lean muscle and bare, tanned skin. And commitment.

'I guess we should get back to business.' Noah's look was cast with dry humour.

'Ready when you are.' Erika prepared to take notes, distracted when there was a knock on the door and Jenny bustled in with a laden lunch tray.

'Thought you could conduct your meeting over a sandwich and a cup of tea.' Her laughing eyes linked the two medics. 'The fillings are your favourite, Erika. Chicken and avocado on wholemeal. Oh—and some custard kisses one of the patients brought in. Enjoy!' She swept out, her smile very wide.

'Hell's teeth,' Noah said under his breath. 'She thinks she's on to something.'

Erika felt a lick of unease. 'She won't say anything, will she? There's enough speculation about us already.'

'Stop worrying.' Noah bent over the lunch tray. 'Jenny wouldn't have lasted two minutes with me if she weren't discreet where it counts. Now, come on, Doctor,' he urged, offering the plate of sandwiches. 'If we want to stay on the right side of our secretary, I suggest we make some inroads on this tucker.'

'What's the position with Joey?' Despite her scattered emotions, Erika kept her voice under control.

'I let him go home.' Noah selected a sandwich. 'With appropriate instructions. He was going stir-crazy.'

'Understandable. I'll follow through, then, when the results of the tests come back. And, if it should turn out to be Lyme disease, I'd like to consult with a parasitologist.'

He nodded. 'Thought you might. Professor Carl Reynolds is our Queensland expert. You'll find his details on the computer. You could e-mail him.'

'Tara?' Erika bit hungrily into her sandwich.

Noah frowned. 'I'd suggest we keep her a few extra days. She needs to be well on her feet before tackling motherhood as well as the farm work. And Michael can't be much help at the moment. The farm is taking all his energies.'

Erika made a note. 'James?'

Noah's mouth turned down. 'I've a call in to his GP. He hasn't got back to me yet. But at least Jamie's job is safe. I've had a word with his employer.'

'He should be able to come off the drip this afternoon,' Erika decided. 'And what about his re-education? Have you suggested anything to him?'

'Not in any great depth.' He sent her a dry look. 'I got the impression he'd rather speak to you.'

Erika sent him a warning look. 'Just don't say anything, Noah!'

'Hey!' He held up his hands in mock surrender. 'Don't shoot the messenger.'

There was a palpable silence. Erika felt all thumbs as she busied herself pouring the tea. 'Any new patients?'

'No. But don't start doing cartwheels,' he said drily. 'It's only Monday yet.'

Erika snapped her diary shut. 'Is this a good time to run something past you?'

'As any.' He looked mildly amused. 'Fire away.'

'I'd like to do something practical for the older folk in the district, particularly the women. Some of them appear quite isolated for various reasons.'

'Are you thinking of something health-related?'

'Well, certainly not bingo! For a start, I thought a low-impact exercise class might appeal to them.'

'And who would conduct the sessions?' Noah's bottom lip rolled in conjecture. 'We're isolated to some degree ourselves. You can't just pull a suitable name out of the *Yellow Pages*.'

'Oh, ye of little faith!' She grinned. 'I'd do the classes myself. I have the grounding.' Almost absently she opened her diary, and let the pages flutter past her fingers. 'At one time I thought I might have had the opportunity to specialise in geriatric care. It was something I really wanted to do.'

Noah looked speculatively at her. 'When was this?'

Erika shrugged. 'A while ago now. I actually applied to a university in the States. A post-grad course they were offering in gerontology.' Her mouth turned down. 'I never heard back, so I guess I missed out.'

Noah felt his heart thud uncomfortably. 'You're not fudging about the commitment you've made here, Erika?'

'How could you even think that?' she protested. 'I've decided to stay. I can't be clearer than that.'

'If we're putting our cards on the table,' Noah said carefully, 'what are you intending to do about the boyfriend?'

Erika stiffened, the tiny gold flecks in her brown eyes sparking battle. 'I'll handle it, Noah. All right?'

'Do that.' His eyes narrowed on her flushed face, the angry tilt of her small chin. 'And soon. I don't want him hovering between us like some kind of spectre.'

Noah glared down into the liquid in his cup. Had he gone too far? Probably. But this time he intended to fight for what he wanted. And he wanted Erika Somers. And that, he thought ruefully, possibly made him slightly crazy. He'd known her such a short time, but already she'd stirred such powerful feelings in him, imbued him with a light-heartedness he'd thought had vanished along with Justine all those months ago.

Erika felt the gooseflesh on her arms with a prickle of alarm. Was it possible Noah Jameson was jealous of Alistair? She gave a silent grimace.

Why was nothing in this world ever straightforward?

Noah lifted his eyes to glance at her, as if alerted by her covert attention. 'What?'

She lifted a shoulder, disguising a wad of confusion. 'Just wondered if we could get back to my original question.' She hurried on. 'We've a large back verandah here I could use for the classes. All I'd need is a powerpoint for my CD player.'

'You'd do it in your own time?' Noah appeared to be considering the implications.

'Once you're back, I could manage it easily.'

He frowned. 'I don't want you spreading yourself too thinly, Erika.'

'I won't.' She swallowed a laugh. 'So, is it OK if I try?'

'OK.' He took a deep breath and let it out slowly. 'I can't see any reason why not.'

'Lovely.' She stood shakily to her feet, the slight air of tension broken. 'I can start putting my plans into action, then.'

They walked outside to Reception together.

'Noah, you can't leave yet.' Jenny was just putting the phone down, her face set in serious lines.

'Don't tell me.' Noah held up both hands in mock resignation. 'My flight's delayed.'

'No.' Jenny placed her hands on the counter in front of her, as if to take comfort from its solidness. 'There's been an accident. Clem Eldridge is in trouble with his tractor.'

'Has he rolled it?' Erika snapped to attention, her thoughts leaping ahead.

'Apparently not.' Jenny shook her head. 'But he's brought down power lines.'

'Bloody hell!' Noah looked at his secretary in disbelief. 'Has the ambulance gone out, Jen?'

'On their way, but they want a doctor at the scene. It all sounds a bit iffy. It could be some time before a crew from the Electrical Authority can get there to make the area safe.' She looked between Noah and Erika and made a little grimace. 'It seems they have to bring in a special flying gang, and they're kilometres away on another job.'

The phone rang again and Noah snapped up the receiver. 'Let's hope it's State Emergency,' he said. 'They'll know exactly what's going on.'

'Poor old Clem.' Jenny shook her head. 'Iris found him a while ago, when she went to summon him for lunch. Fortunately, her family recently presented them with a mobile phone. Iris takes it everywhere with her.'

So, she'd been able to summon help quite quickly, by the sound of it. Erika felt the nerves in her stomach clench. Electrocution. The word had a terrible finality about it.

'OK.' Noah replaced the receiver, his face grim. 'Here's the position as we know it.'

Instinctively, Jenny clutched Erika's arm, the intensity of his manner drawing them together like birds sheltering from a storm.

'Clem had been ploughing his north paddock.'

Noah's hands came up to bracket his head. 'It seems because he hadn't cultivated it in a couple of years it was rough going.'

Jenny bit her lip. 'And he's never been exactly gentle with machinery...'

'Quite,' Noah confirmed with a grimace. 'He's gone too close to a dividing fence and struck a power pole. It had been eaten by white ants at the base, making it unstable.'

'Has it fallen on him?' Erika was almost afraid to ask the question.

'On the tractor's cabin.' Noah spoke abruptly. 'Miraculously, the rubber tyres are keeping him insulated. But he's injured, and anchored there until we can get the power switched off.'

Erika's hand went to her throat. 'Are you saying the area's live?'

'Within about a metre.' Noah's look was grim. 'And we'd better get cracking.' Wheeling round, he began striding back to his consulting room.

Erika set out after him.

'I'll call ambulance control, shall I?' Jenny called. 'Tell them you're on the way?'

Without turning, Noah lifted a hand in acknowledgement. 'We'll stop by the hospital,' he snapped to Erika, and began locking drawers and cabinets. 'We'll need a trauma kit. Better collect a couple of waterproofs as well. The Eldridge farm is high up. If there's rain about, you can bet your boots it'll fall there.'

Erika looked ruefully at her bronze suede trousers and pale linen shirt. Hardly the thing to wear to an accident scene. But that was the least of her concerns. 'I've a windcheater in the car.'

'Get it.' Noah was on the move again, streaming orders to Jenny. 'Call my mother, will you? Let her know about the change of plan. There should be a charter flight out later tonight. I'll hitch a ride on that.' He held the door open with his boot. 'Call on the mobile if there's an emergency, Jen. One of us will come back.' In an aside to Erika, he said gravely. 'What a luxury, having two doctors. Your blood's worth bottling, Erika Somers.'

Erika hooked her coat off the passenger seat of her car, feeling warmed through and through. She had an incredible sense of belonging, and a certainty she'd done the right thing in deciding to stay here and to throw her lot in with Noah.

'We'll have to step on it, Erika.' Noah reversed the Land Rover in a swift arc, and within seconds they had left the hospital and the town proper behind.

Erika turned her face towards the ribbon of country road. The thick brush of lantana came almost to the edges, a frame for the rolling hills and peeling gum trees. 'Do we know how badly Clem's injured?' she asked.

'The SES boys think he's caught some of the weight of the power pole across his shoulder. Missed his head, fortunately. And no doubt he'll be suffering shock.' Noah's dark brows drew together. 'I didn't want to make things more dramatic in front of Jenny, but Iris has her two grandchildren for the day.'

Erika caught her breath. 'Are they at the scene?'

'Seems so. They're around five and four,' he said. 'Old enough to be quite severely traumatised.'

Erika glanced at her watch and thought about the scenario they were facing. 'I'm on a steep learning curve here to some extent, Noah. What's the plan?'

'I guess much will depend on how soon the area is made safe.' He gunned the motor and they began to climb higher.

Erika felt the nerves in her stomach react. This looked like wild country, all bony ridges and wind-blown tussocks.

'We may have to consider pain relief orally.' Noah's voice was clipped. 'That's if we can get close enough with safety.'

'That's a big "if", isn't it?' She swung to him with a look of scepticism.

'Perhaps.' He swung the Land Rover through the farm gates, the big tyres rattling over the metal grid.

To Erika's relief the State Emergency people were already at the scene, and within seconds Noah was nosing his vehicle in beside the bright yellow ones belonging to the rescue team.

Grabbing her bag, she was out in a flash, trying to get her bearings. The tension in the air was palpable.

And no wonder. Erika stood in stunned horror. Another hundred metres up the hill a grey tractor was skewed into the fence, imprisoned by a band of sparking wires.

'Helluva situation, Doc,' Pete Delgado, the ambulance officer, said in an undertone. 'I can't get any sense out of Iris at all. She won't budge.'

Shading her eyes, Erika looked to where the woman stood like a slab of petrified rock, the two children beside her just as still. To Erika's trained eye, it was apparent they were all suffering varying degrees of trauma.

She took off in a run.

'Erika!' Noah's bark was like a whiplash, hauling her to a stop. 'Where do you think you're going?'

Resentment crowded in on her. How dared he bawl her out in front of everyone?

'I'm seeing to Iris and the children...'

'Not without a guide, you're not!'

Feet dragging, she made her way back to the assembled group.

'I know your natural response is to want to help.' Noah's blue gaze struck an arc across the space between them. 'But let's just see what we can do safely, shall we?'

Erika's cheeks were on fire. She'd reacted like an over-enthusiastic med student.

'The responsibility for a successful outcome depends entirely on everyone's co-operation.' Tom Sigley, the team leader from the State Emergency

Service, looked measuredly at the company. 'Hopefully, a fly gang of workmen will be here soon, to disconnect the power. But they've had to be recalled from another job so we're a bit hamstrung until they get here.'

'Where's the transformer located?' Noah sought to get to the nub of the issue.

'Up near the house.' Tom chewed on his bottom lip. 'They'll alert us as soon as it's inactive.'

'Can I get close enough to at least ask Clem how he is?'

Erika felt a lurching sensation in her stomach. Hadn't Noah heard *anything* Tom Sigley had said?

'I suppose…' The SES leader too looked doubtful. 'As long as you follow my instructions to the letter.'

'Will do. Erika?' With his hand on her arm, Noah drew her away from the group. 'We'll need to wear special gear for this junket,' he told her, faint lines of strain arrowing into the corners of his mouth.

Erika licked her lips. She presumed he meant the thick overalls and insulated boots the emergency people were wearing. It was all shaping up as much more complicated than she'd envisaged. Nevertheless…

'I need to get to Iris and the children, Noah.' Her voice was clearly determined as she pulled on the orange-coloured overalls.

'I know.' Noah dipped his head into the rear of the emergency vehicle and emerged with a pair of thick-soled boots. 'Here, these look about your size. You attend to Iris and the kids and I'll see what I can make of Clem's condition. OK?'

Erika was tight-lipped. Even with insulated clothing, Noah's safety couldn't be guaranteed. She was only guessing, but the downed lines had to be generating enough volts to flatten a herd of elephants—let alone a man.

She touched his hands. 'You'll wear insulated gloves as well, won't you? And a helmet?'

'Yes, Doctor.' A wry smile twisted his mouth.

'I'm not joking, Noah.' Her lips pressed down in disapproval. 'Heroes have a limited lifespan.'

'Heroines too, Erika.' His eyes glinted. 'How do you think I felt seeing you haring off up the hill to Iris?'

She blinked. 'I know—that was foolish.'

Noah swung up one of the trauma kits and handed her the other one. 'Try to get Iris and the kids back down here to base. At least then you'll be able to keep an eye on them for post-trauma signs. There's no guarantee how long we'll be here, so there'll be food and hot drinks laid on as well.' He turned as Tom Sigley approached.

'If you're ready, Noah, we'll make tracks up to Clem.'

'Right. Who's taking Erika?'

'I've assigned Kyle Matthews.' Tom gave a signal to the young man watching keenly from a short distance away.

They moved off in different directions, but for

a fleeting moment Erika looked back, an odd headiness catching her by surprise. Take care of him, please, she prayed silently.

'Let's hope no one gets zapped, eh, Doc?' Kyle touched the gold stud in his ear. 'We'll all be in strife big time if a storm breaks. Water and electricity don't mix at all.'

Well she knew that! Erika felt unnerved, casting a glance at the ragged grey clouds suspended above them. The wind too had risen, bending the ironbark saplings, sending their lonely rustling up and down the hillside.

'Not much further.' The young volunteer gave her an encouraging grin and they quickened their pace.

'Mrs Eldridge? Iris…' Erika was close enough to call gently. 'I'm the doctor, Erika Somers. Will you let me help you?'

Iris Eldridge showed no sign of having heard, staring at the tractor, her hands clutching the mobile phone to her chest.

'Grandma won't move.' The older child, a little girl, held out a hand tremulously towards Erika.

'Oh, baby…' Erika dropped to the children's level, scooping them to her side. 'What's your name, sweetheart?'

The little chin trembled. 'Victoria Eldridge.'

'And is this your brother?' Erika smoothed a hand over the fine blonde head.

She nodded. 'He's Brodie Eldridge. Is Grandpa going to die?'

Two sets of blue eyes looked fearfully at Erika. 'Oh—darlings, no!' Hugging them, she let her gaze track to where Noah and Tom stood in seeming consultation a short distance from the tractor. She'd have to try to explain to them.

'Do you see all the men in orange clothes?' she began. 'Well, they've come to help your grandpa. And pretty soon some workmen will come too, and turn off the power switch. Like that!' Erika clicked her fingers for effect. 'And we'll all be as safe as can be.'

At that moment Erika heard the stifled moan behind her, spinning around just in time to see Kyle catch Iris before she hit the ground. Releasing the youngsters, she leapt to the woman's side. 'Lay her down carefully,' she cautioned, nodding in approval when Kyle gently placed Iris on her left side and drew her right leg into a bent-knee position.

'I've done level-two first aid,' he enlightened her, with quiet confidence.

'Good work, Kyle.' Erika gave her approval.

'Will Granny die?' Like small creatures seeking the reassurance of an adult, the children clung to Erika's side.

She was horrified. These poor little mites seemed obsessed with death and dying. 'Granny will be fine,' she said. 'She's just fainted.'

Erika prayed it was nothing more sinister. But with Iris's age nothing could be automatically ruled out. A stroke or heart attack were also possibilities.

Concentrating, she timed Iris's pulse, and then with swift precision whipped the blood pressure cuff around her arm. Her mouth drew in. One hundred over sixty-five. A touch low—which, combined with her rapid pulse, would seem to indicate a faint.

'Let's get Mrs Eldridge on oxygen, please, Kyle.' Erika delved into the trauma kit for a pen torch. So far so good, she thought, when Iris's pupils appeared equal and reacting.

Just then Iris stirred and opened her eyes. She looked stunned for a moment, before two large tears tracked slowly down her cheeks. 'Coot of a man,' she murmured, and closed her eyes again.

'You'll be OK, Mrs E.' With great gentleness Kyle slipped the oxygen mask into place, letting his large hand rest briefly on the grandmother's faded blonde hair.

CHAPTER EIGHT

NOAH had been aware of her approach. He took a breath, its rough expulsion laced with frustration. The whole rescue caper was dragging on far longer than he'd bargained for. Eyes narrowed, he watched Tom pocket his mobile phone.

'They still can't give us an ETA, Doc.'

'Get that insulating device you mentioned, then, Tom. I'm not waiting any longer.'

'Noah?'

Twisting his head, he gave Erika a questioning look. 'What's this, a deputation?'

Erika stood her ground. 'Iris is fretting about Clem. I told her I'd find out what's happening.'

'Not a lot, as you can see. How's Iris?'

'Resting in the ambulance. I've just taken her off the oxygen.'

'And the kids?'

'They'll be fine. Their parents have just arrived. They heard about Clem's accident on the car radio. Nearly went frantic until they could see for themselves what happened. How is Clem?' Erika's gaze homed in on where the farmer's head was just a silver-grey blur through the splintered window of the tractor's cabin.

Noah drew in a long breath and let it go. 'Everything points to a dislocated shoulder. And he's feeling sick…'

Erika stared at him. 'There's something else?'

'He has a history of mild angina. It's just another complication.'

The scenario they were faced with hit Erika like a lead weight. 'You're going to try to give the medication to him orally, aren't you?'

'I don't see I have a choice.' Noah frowned. 'In his exhausted state, the last thing he needs is a bout of vomiting.'

'Surely the power people can't be much longer?' Erika's hair brushed against his shoulder as she swung towards him.

'They're on the way. That's all we know.' With steady hands Noah prepared the drugs.

Erika felt her throat tighten. 'What will you give him?'

'Morphine syrup, five milligrams,' Noah said shortly. 'I realise it's a relatively light dose, but I don't want to upset his stomach any more than it is already.'

Erika gnawed at her lip. So, of course he would add an anti-emetic, and hope to heaven it kept the morphine down. They both knew it was a gamble. But, as Noah rightly pointed out, it was the only option available.

Noah secured the medication in a plastic container, small enough to pass through the jagged opening in the tractor's windshield, simple enough for Clem to grasp and swallow the contents.

'Be here, Erika—in case you're needed.'

Erika beat back a sudden pang of alarm. 'Just be careful.' Her hand went briefly to his arm.

His mouth dipped into a lopsided grin. 'My will's at the local solicitor's.'

Erika looked at him, appalled. How could he be so flippant, when she was dying a thousand small deaths at the thought of what he was intending to do?

'Just make sure you get back here in one piece,' she threatened softly. 'Or I'll maim you.' She turned, her eyes widening in disbelief when Tom produced the insulating device. Nothing more than a stick made of fibreglass.

'That should do it.' Slowly and carefully, Tom's broad fingers taped the medication to one end of the stick. He sliced the tape neatly. 'Now, you know what to do, Noah?'

'I know what to do,' Noah reassured the SES chief quietly. 'And thanks for your co-operation, Tom.'

What if something awful happened? Erika's heart felt like a jackhammer against her ribs as she watched Noah approach his patient. Step by careful step.

Her breath spun out in a tight sigh. It was useless telling herself he'd taken every precaution. Accidents could and did still happen, as swiftly as taking a breath...

Inch by inch Noah moved closer to his target. Fearing for him, praying for him, she hardly dared breathe, her senses heightening almost to breaking point. And all about her the world seemed to have shrunk, become shot with unnatural stillness, a breathlessness, the only movement on the hillside the slight bowing of the tree shadows.

'That's far enough!' Tom Sigley's snapped command sent Erika's hand to her mouth.

And then it was done. Clem had swallowed his painkiller and Noah was reversing his steps, backing away from the crackling powerlines slowly, gingerly. Until he was well away, striding to safety.

Erika's arms ached to reach out to him, to hold him, but sanity prevailed. 'Well done,' she said quietly. 'Let's hope he can keep it down.'

'Yes.' A steely glint invaded Noah's eyes for an instant, before he handed the equipment back to Tom.

Accepting it, Tom merely nodded, his mouth compressing.

Emotions began clogging Erika's throat. There was a quiet dignity about these bush people, an inbuilt instinct to help where they could when one of their own was in trouble. A sudden warmth shot through her. With an optimism born of happiness, she knew she had more than a fair chance of being totally accepted into this small community.

She had no time to become too introspective. At Noah's request, she'd made her way back to base, to reassure Iris about her husband's condition.

Iris had perked up considerably, insisting she

was quite able to assist dispensing the hot drinks and food to the team of volunteers. Erika had other ideas, guessing the woman's keep-busy philosophy was simply to help her cope with the uncertainty.

'Coot of a man,' Iris snorted. 'Causing all this trouble…'

Only Erika noticed the slight clenching of the older woman's fingers as she proffered the mugs of tea and then jerkily wiped her hands on her apron.

Satisfied there was nothing more she could do for the moment, Erika retraced her steps to Noah.

'Everything OK?' He was carefully monitoring his watch, not looking up.

'As much as it can be.' Erika's sigh came up from her toes. 'It's so hard waiting.'

'It's almost twenty minutes since Clem had his medication,' Noah said with quiet triumph.

'It's looking good, then.' Erika turned her head up. Cloud shadows were brushing the sky, and directly above the mountains they were sagging and heavy. Surely the men would get here soon…

'They're here!' Tom materialised quietly beside the two medics. 'They're at the transformer now.'

Erika could have hugged him. She flung Noah a questioning look. 'Now what?'

'We continue to wait,' he said calmly. 'And watch.'

And it seemed the small world about them was watching too. And expectant. The air around them fairly bristled with suspense, straining towards a climax.

'Oh, Lord…' Erika whispered to the silent trees, as the electrical sparks, bright and white, sputtered and died.

It was as if the starter had fired his pistol. A cheer rang out, reverberated up and down the hillside. Motors were gunned and emergency vehicles fanned out and began racing to the accident scene.

'Stand back.' Noah placed a guiding hand on Erika's shoulder as the crew thrust forward with wrecking bars. Within seconds the doors of the tractor's cabin were spliced through and Clem was being lifted gently out.

'What's the damage, Doc?' The farmer's words were a muffled thread of sound.

Noah looked up from his brief examination. 'You'll live to plough another day, Clem. Erika?' He motioned her to the head of the stretcher.

'Now?' Her eyes widened in query.

'While he's mostly out of it.'

They worked instinctively, Erika steadying the injured man while Noah repositioned the shoulder. 'OK?'

Erika nodded, and braced herself for Clem's little groan as the limb clicked back into place.

'I'll ride back with him,' she said briskly. 'Iris?' She looked round for her other patient.

'Here, Doctor.' Iris stepped forward, her face looking as crumpled as her worn apron.

Erika's heart contracted. Iris looked pale again.

The adrenalin rush that had come with the rescue of her husband had all but faded, and she was exhibiting all the signs of post-trauma plus sheer exhaustion.

'Perhaps you'd like to ride in front with Pete,' Erika said gently, moving to one side to allow Noah to vault out of the ambulance.

'I've given him half an anginine,' he said guardedly. 'Just to be on the safe side.'

Erika nodded, filing the information away in her head. She could only marvel at the co-ordination and the swiftness with which everything had been done, and was still being done. The hillside hummed with activity.

Looking at the sky, she felt a rush of gladness. The dark clouds had miraculously lifted and the skeletal outlines of the ring-barked trees spiked a pink sunset.

'Been a long day, hasn't it?' Noah's mouth pulled down at the corners.

For him it obviously had been, she conceded silently, watching him work his shoulders.

'Are we keeping Iris in overnight?

'*We* are not doing anything, Doctor,' Erika said firmly, something in the way he was looking at her making her catch her breath. 'I'm back on duty and you're away to catch your flight.'

'Am I just?' He sent her a lazy smile, moved closer and asked softly, 'Going to kiss me goodbye?'

She managed a short laugh. 'Not likely. Go.'

She made a little shooing motion with her hand. 'You're on holidays.'

'Scared we'd frighten the horses?'

She rolled her eyes. 'See you in a week, Dr Jameson.'

His eyes lit with devilment. 'Five days,' he countered huskily. 'Big difference.'

Erika felt heat rush to her face, all her resolutions to be thoroughly professional around him running away like sand through a sieve.

'Noah...' His body was very close, his mouth closer. And there was such a need inside her. So much loving she wanted to share.

She glanced quickly around and then pressed her mouth softly to his. 'Now go.' She pushed him determinedly away, spoiling the effect by laughing.

He stepped back, his amused gaze roaming over her flushed cheeks. 'See you,' he said, holding up the fingers of one hand for effect. 'And I'm counting.'

Erika fluttered him a wave as the ambulance doors closed. A glow of pleasure ran right through her, and she was still being warmed by it when they pulled up at the hospital.

Erika made her last notation and put the file away, a sigh of relief whispering through her lips.

Spinning off her chair, she moved to the window, absorbing the stillness of late afternoon, breathing in the faint smell of woodsmoke.

Almost absently, she glanced at her watch, realising it had been twenty-four hours since Noah had left. Closing her eyes, she smiled, losing herself in sweet remembering before raising her arms in an all-encompassing sensuously long stretch.

Reality came back with a snap when Jenny popped her head through the door. 'Could you see Pete Delgado? He doesn't have an appointment.'

'Sure, I'll see him.' Erika flashed a faintly weary smile at the secretary. 'Have to look after our own.'

'Sorry to put this on you so late, Doc.' The ambulance officer, still clad in his teal-blue uniform, sat awkwardly in the chair Erika kept at right angles to her own. 'Fact is, I've been putting it off...'

Erika looked down at his file and smiled. Apart from a tetanus jab, Pete seemed not to have been near a doctor for months. 'You'll get no lectures from me about that, Pete.' Noting the day's date, she turned encouraging to her patient. 'It's not always wise, but it's entirely human. Now, how can I help?'

'It's this thing under my eye,' he said gruffly. 'Every time I look in the mirror to shave, it seems to have got bigger.'

Sensing Pete's tension, Erika swung off her chair. 'Let's have a look, then, shall we?' With as little fuss as possible she settled him under the examination light.

After her thorough examination she frowned. The lump was there, all right, clearly visible under the left eye, squishy to the touch. 'How long have you had it, would you say, Pete?' she asked, scanning the eyeball for anything untoward. It seemed clear.

'A few months. It came up red on the lower lid and then went away. Then soon after I noticed the lump.' His throat rippled uncomfortably as he swallowed. 'It's not—cancer, is it?'

At once Erika had the cause of Pete Delgado's fears, and the misguided reason he'd procrastinated about seeing a doctor. The common belief that what you didn't know couldn't hurt you. Just drive you slowly up the wall. Of course, with his health-related training he should have known better. But it was easy to lose objectivity when your own health was involved.

'I'd say there's very little chance it's cancer, Pete.' Erika turned to the basin to wash her hands.

His shoulders slumped with relief. 'What is it, then, Doc?'

Erika took up her own chair again, pulling her referral pad towards her. 'Quite possibly, it's something called a chalazion.'

His eyebrows peaked. 'A what?'

Erika smiled. 'In simple terms, a kind of sty that goes inwards. There's gunk in there—not problematic, but for cosmetic purposes you should have it seen to. There'll be some quite delicate surgery involved. If you lived in Melbourne I'd trot you along to see my dad.'

'Eye specialist, is he?' Pete's dark eyes regarded her shyly.

'Big time.' Erika began writing.

'He must be proud of you, then? Being a doctor as well, I mean,' Pete clarified.

Erika's mouth twisted into a wry little moue. 'Here's your referral, Pete,' she sidetracked smoothly. 'It's to Tim Pacey in Warwick. You'll need to phone his office for an appointment. I understand he visits every fortnight from Brisbane. Does a clinic and so on.'

'Will he do it straight away?' Pete looked down at the sealed envelope in his hand.

'Hmm—possibly not. He may just examine you and then schedule your surgery. It's day surgery,' she emphasised. 'Probably take about an hour. And you'll have your eye covered afterwards, so take someone with you to drive you home.'

The ambulance officer nodded. 'Mirry'll come with me,' he said, mentioning his wife. Getting to his feet, he paused. 'The specialist—he'll send a sample to be analysed, will he?'

'Don't be alarmed.' Erika stood quickly and walked to the door with him. It was apparent Pete Delgado's fears were not entirely laid to rest. 'It's a routine procedure.' She smiled. 'And let me know how you get on.'

'You're staying with us, then? I heard a rumour.'

'Yes, I'm staying,' she said, hugging the knowledge sweetly to her.

'That's mighty news.' Retreating with a grin, he turned and opened the door. 'Wait'll I tell the lads.'

Her mouth still wearing a little smile, Erika

wrote up Pete Delgado's file, her mind savouring the words. *I'm staying.* Life was looking pretty good, she thought, locking the drugs cabinet and tidying the top of her desk. And she'd write to Alistair tonight and tell him she couldn't marry him…

'Could you authorise and sign a couple of things, Erika?' Jenny walked in, juggling the mail. 'Oh, and this just came overnight express for you.' She laid the priority-paid packet on the desk in front of Erika.

Erika lifted a shoulder. 'Probably bills,' she grimaced, noting her father's bold writing on the envelope. 'I think my car registration is about due.'

Jenny made a face. 'Another week's pay down the tubes. Would you like to make up a foursome for tennis tonight?' she asked, hitching herself across the corner of the desk.

Erika sighed. 'I'd love to, Jen, but I'm really beat. And I've still to do a ward round. Ask me again next week,' she smiled.

'You bet I will.' Jenny slid off the desk, grinning. 'We're keeping you as Hillcrest's secret weapon for when the fixtures start.' She waggled her fingers. 'Night, then. See you tomorrow.'

At the hospital, Erika called first on Clem Eldridge. He'd recovered with no ill effects and she was about to sign his release. 'No high jinks, now, Mr Eldridge,' she warned, running her stethoscope over him for a final check. 'I want you to take it easy for the next little while, OK?'

'I'll see he does what you've told him, Dr Somers.' Iris, who was sitting patiently by her husband's bed, placed her hand firmly on his arm.

'A man knows when he's beaten.' Clem looked up ruefully from under bushy brows. 'My son reckons I'm to stay off the tractor as well...'

Iris shook her head. 'I've been telling him, Doctor, it's time we took a bit of a holiday. Brian and Tracey are quite capable of running things. Brian's done a degree in agriculture, you know,' she said proudly.

'Then I'm sure he's more than capable.' Erika bit back a smile. Folding her stethoscope, she slid it into her top pocket. 'And if you phone him now, he can come and collect you.'

With the Eldridges' thanks still ringing in her ears and warming her heart, Erika went to find James. He was in the lounge, dealing himself a hand of patience. Glancing up, he sent her a wry grin. 'Bit bored at the moment, Doc.'

'Well, that's a good sign.' Eyeing him amusedly, Erika sat down beside him. 'How are you feeling?'

'Great. Terrific. And I've done everything you said. Looked at the video, read some stuff, and Nurse Bryson's shown me how to plan my diet.'

'That's good.' Erika flicked open his chart. 'What accommodation do you have at the farm?'

'A caravan. And it's OK. Warm and dry, if

that's what you're worried about!' He grinned cheekily.

Erika pursed her lips and looked down at the notes. Jamie Cosgrove had recovered quickly and without complications, and from what she'd observed herself he was jumping out of his skin. 'All right, young man.' She smiled. 'I'm going to let you go. How are you getting back to the farm?'

He coloured. 'I've given Lisa the use of my car. I'll ring her to come and get me.'

'Good.' Erika dug a card out of her pocket. 'And if you get into any strife healthwise, ring this mobile number. Either Dr Jameson or I will be on call.'

The young man nodded and swallowed. 'Thanks Dr Somers. I won't scare myself like that again, though.'

'I'm glad to hear it.' Erika got to her feet. 'Now, get some food in, James, and look after yourself, OK?' She touched him on the shoulder. 'And I'm very pleased you're well again.'

It was almost eight o'clock by the time Erika arrived home. *If you could see me now, Noah.* She smiled inwardly, setting her takeaway spaghetti bolognaise on the counter.

As far as meals went in the future, she would really have to get her act together, she thought ruefully. Begin making some casseroles to freeze and keeping the ingredients on hand for a quick stir-fry.

Hungrily, she set about her meal, and it wasn't until she'd finished and settled over her coffee that she remembered the mail she'd pushed into her bag.

Slicing open the overnight express packet, she found the letter her father had obviously sent on. Blinking uncertainly at the Chicago postmark, she felt her heart begin to pound. With shaking fingers she tore open the envelope.

'Oh, my God...' she whispered a smile of unbelief clinging to her mouth as she read and reread the contents of the letter. It was the chance she'd been waiting for.

But how on earth was she going to tell Noah...?

CHAPTER NINE

SATURDAY morning.

Erika heard his voice long before she'd expected to. He was back early. And she could hardly find the words to tell him what she had to.

'Hi!' His dark head came round her door, his smile radiating a hundred-watt brilliance. 'Jen tells me it's only a short list. I'll take half and then we'll talk. OK?'

'OK.' Erika's smile was a travesty of indecision. She swallowed. 'Would you like your office back?' Lifting her bag she prepared to vacate.

'Stay there.' He waved a hand dismissively. 'I'll use the second room. Besides...' His grin was slow and wound itself right around her heart. 'You look good in here. Right at home, if I may say so?'

It was only as Erika saw her last patient out that she gave in to the terrible churning in her stomach. What if Noah chose not to understand? she fretted. She clicked her tongue in self-exasperation. He wouldn't be so dog-in-the-manger, surely...

His rat-a-tat on the door put paid to her wild conjecture. She held herself tightly as he came in. With a flick of his hand, he lobbed a folder on her desk.

'All clear?' Moving towards her, he swooped

and lifted her out of her chair. 'Miss me?' he prompted softly, tipping her chin up with his fingers and searching her eyes.

'Yes.' She laughed a little shakily. 'I missed you.'

'Me too—missed you,' he murmured, before his mouth found hers.

A soft little mewl whimpered out of her throat and she swayed towards him, her fingers tangling in the darkness of his hair.

Passion. Was this what he'd meant? In all the times Alistair had kissed her it had never felt like this. A delicious ache began coiling deep inside her; her blood was clamouring. And their kisses went on and on.

Finally, Noah pulled back, burying his face in the softness of her hair, his hands cradling the narrow curve of her hip.

She is so beautiful, he thought, sliding his hands up under her loose top and drawing a sharp breath as he touched the bare skin of her waist.

'Noah...' Erika drew out his name on a quivery breath, looking deeply into his eyes. The warmth of his kiss was still flooding through her. It might be too soon to call it love, but what else could it be...?

She raised her hands to her face, becoming dizzily aware of the door opening and the figure there.

'Coffee?' Jenny's voice broke the spell surrounding them.

'Ah—thanks, Jen.' Noah stepped away quickly,

deliberately shielding Erika from the other's view. 'Why don't you shoot off now?' he said, ramming both hands through his hair. 'We'll lock up.'

With Jenny gone, he let out a long breath. 'This is getting ridiculous,' he growled.

Erika managed a shaken laugh. 'You have to admit her timing's perfect.'

'A perfect nuisance,' he countered, drawing her slowly against him. 'You're shaking,' he said, holding her close.

'So are you,' she replied, muffled into his shoulder.

'Coffee, then?'

'Perhaps we'd better.'

With the coffee poured, Erika took her mug and walked to the window, looking out as if to imprint every last nuance on her mind.

The early afternoon lay drowsing, the faintest breeze nudging the long, pale leaves of the eucalypts into a quaint dancing rhythm.

She glanced at her watch. Time was running out and she had to talk to Noah...

'I want you to take a look at this.' He was holding out the folder he'd brought in earlier.

She gave him a quick smile. 'What is it?'

'I've had a partnership agreement drawn up.'

'Oh—'

'It's relatively simple,' he said. 'Straightforward. Nevertheless, I'd like you to read it over the weekend and we can co-sign it on Monday.' He sent her a wry grin. 'I'm sure Jenny will be more than pleased to act as witness.'

Her heart skittering, Erika hardly glanced at the papers before placing them back on the desk. 'Noah—we have to talk. I'm not in a position to come in as a partner—at least not yet. But I'm really grateful and—touched you've gone to all this trouble.'

His dark brows drew together. 'You've lost me. What do you mean you're not in a position to come in as a partner? If it's money—?'

'No.' Erika shook her head, swallowing the dryness in her throat. This was turning out far more difficult than she'd imagined. 'The fact is, I've been accepted at Loyola University in Chicago. The course I told you about. It's the chance of a lifetime. I'll have access to some of the best people in the field.'

Noah stood, arms folded, and stared at her.

'Noah?' She gave a stilted laugh. 'Say something.'

His expression darkened. 'Congratulations, then. Will that do? So, you're going to specialise after all.' His tone was bitter. 'Your father must be pleased. Is he paying your way as well?'

'No, he is not!' A feeling of nausea twisted inside her. 'I pay my own way. And, yes, my father is pleased for me. That's not a major crime, is it?'

Noah paced away, turning to glare at her. 'I cannot believe my naivety. My total lack of judgement in allowing myself to get involved all over again with another career junkie.'

He might as well have struck her. Erika's face crumpled with pain. 'That's not fair, Noah! The course is for three months!' Her voice rose. 'I fully intend coming back to Hillcrest.'

His look was hard. 'You won't be back, Erika. Once you've been exposed to that kind of intensive learning it will be like an aphrodisiac. You'll want more and more.' His mouth twisted. 'And "Erika Somers, *geriatrician*" has quite a ring to it, doesn't it?'

Erika felt as though her heart was splitting in two. She closed her eyes briefly and then forced herself to look at him. 'Aren't you rather judging me, Noah?' she said quietly. 'I'm not Justine. And I will be back.'

'The hell you will.' Pretending not to see the raw hurt on her face he bent and unlocked the desk drawer, pulling out a chequebook. Slapping it on the desk, he swung back into his chair.

Shocked, sick to her stomach, Erika could only stare at him, finally taking the cheque with trembling hands. 'Thank you.' She dipped her head. 'I've left everything in order.'

His mouth hardened. 'When do you leave?'

'Today.' She gave a little shake of her head, trying to clear the fog that seemed to be clouding her brain. 'I'm booked on a Brisbane-Los Angeles flight at noon tomorrow. Then connect with another domestic flight to Chicago. The course starts almost immediately.' And why was she telling him any of this? she fretted sickeningly. He didn't want to know. Couldn't have cared less if she was flying on a broomstick to the States.

'You'll be a busy girl, then, won't you?' Noah put his pen back into his shirt pocket and straightened out of his chair.

'Noah...' she paused, blinking. His facial muscles were taut, his skin pale under his tan. Oh, dear God. She licked her lips. 'I wondered whether I could leave some stuff here, until I make other arrangements?'

Their gazes locked for a long time. 'To my knowledge no one's using the flat,' he said, and then he turned and walked out. She did not see him again.

Erika nosed her Laser into the car park and stopped beside Noah's. It was three months almost to the day since she'd left.

Cutting the engine, she blocked a wide yawn. She'd been flying for hours out of one time zone and into another, arriving back in the country only that morning. And, although it probably hadn't been a good idea healthwise, she'd reclaimed her car from the long-term parking facility at the airport and immediately set out on the three-hour drive to Hillcrest.

Her stomach was churning at the thought of confronting Noah. But, on the other hand, perhaps she wouldn't have to. She could collect the key to the flat from Jenny, gather up her belongings and be gone before he'd even know she'd come back.

That her heart was still breaking over him was something she had yet to come to terms with.

Sighing, she glanced at her watch and saw it was noon. And there were still patients' cars and utilities parked all around the surgery. A small frown creased her forehead. Either Noah had been called to an emergency or the Saturday morning surgery was running impossibly behind schedule.

And it's none of my business, she reminded herself grimly. Forcing the might-have-been hopes to the back of her mind, she climbed stiffly from the car and stretched, shivering in the sudden chilly gust of wind.

The sun made a dappled pattern through the trees as she made her way around to the rear entrance. Her nerves shredding, she walked up the ramp and pulled open the screen door.

'Erika!' Jenny emerged from the small utility room, surprise widening her eyes to saucers.

'Hello, Jen.' Erika let the door swing shut behind her. 'OK if I come in?'

The two women stared awkwardly at each other, and then Erika took the initiative. 'I've come for my gear. I wondered if I could get the key to the flat?'

'You left one of your white coats behind too.' Jenny seemed suddenly to come to life, beckoning Erika to the second consulting room. 'I had it dry-cleaned.'

'Oh—thanks.' Erika followed the secretary inside. 'You're a gem.' She gave a faltering glance around the soft lilac of the walls. All the way from the Brisbane airport she'd had a sense of coming home... 'Surgery still going on?' She threw the query a bit stiltedly at Jenny.

'Mmm.' Jenny made a small face. 'Flu bug everywhere in the district. Noah's out on his feet. I told him he should think of getting a revolving door put in,' she quipped darkly. 'Erika...' Her sudden little moue was full of conjecture. 'I suppose you couldn't—?'

'No!' Erika was adamant. 'I know what you're about to ask, Jenny, and the answer is no!'

'Look.' Jenny plonked herself determinedly on the corner of the desk. 'I've no idea what happened between you two, and Noah's been about as communicative as a thumbtack. And about as sharp,' she added aggrievedly.

'Jenny...' Erika's voice shook fractionally. 'There's nothing I can tell you. And I should be on my way. I have no business here.'

'Who says so?' It was an explosion of utter frustration. 'All I know is that there are patients waiting to be seen. House-calls to be made. Ward rounds to do. And you're here and available. You've even a clean white coat,' she threw in triumphantly.

Erika's heart revved. Jenny McGill really knew how to put the pressure on. But dared she help out?

Apart from the ethics of it all, Erika herself felt far from fresh...

'How many patients are there?' she asked, thinking it could just possibly qualify as her last goodwill gesture towards Noah. And he could hardly sack her.

'About ten...*ish*,' Jenny amended vaguely, her grin appealingly innocent. 'Can I wheel in the first one?'

'I suppose so.' Erika's capitulation was decidedly hollow. 'Just give me a few minutes to get my head straight. And a cup of tea wouldn't go astray either,' she added darkly.

Thank God. An hour and a half later, and with some relief, Erika saw her last patient out. Collapsing back on to her chair, she slumped wearily at the desk, massaging the dull ache away from her temples.

'Just who gave you permission to treat my patients?' The door was flung open and Noah stood there, his whole bearing bristling with indignation.

Slowly and deliberately, Erika raised her eyes. And her faint hope that his attitude towards her might have softened flickered and died.

'What on earth possessed you?' he continued, his word slashing harshly between them.

Dull depression settled on Erika like a cloud. 'Just get down off your high horse, Noah,' she managed flatly. 'I was merely trying to do you a favour.'

'Slumming, were you?' His smile became a grim twist. 'I don't understand your reasoning at all.'

Erika could feel the shaking in her knees as she got to her feet. 'But then you haven't actually tried to, have you?'

'Are you here to collect your things?' With several strides he moved into the consulting room and across to the window.

'Yes,' she said stiffly. 'And thank you again for allowing me to leave them here.'

He lifted a shoulder. 'It was hardly a problem.'

'Well, I appreciated it anyway.' She shrugged out of her white coat. 'Where do you want me to leave the keys to the flat?'

'Wherever.' With a jagged sigh he turned and leaned his shoulder against the window. He felt grim, and it was all such a mess. Her hurt little face had been haunting him for the past three months, and now, when he had the chance to try to sort things out—a chance she'd handed him on a platter—he'd gone and made things a thousand times worse.

'Erika—' He stared at her, his jaw working. 'Let's at least end this with some civility. Why don't I buy you a drink later? You can return the keys to me then.'

Erika opened her mouth, the words to refuse outright lodging uncomfortably in her throat. Long drawn-out farewells were not her style, but he looked so jaded and fed up. Her resolve weakened. 'Where?'

'The pub? But I can't make it until later this afternoon, I'm afraid.' He rubbed wearily at the back of his neck. 'I've several house-calls to make, including one out to the Petanis.'

Erika felt a stab of alarm. 'It's not the baby, is it?'

He shook his head. 'It's Tara. King-sized dose of this flu, by the sound of it. She's in a bit of a panic. Wondering should she continue nursing and whether the baby's getting enough milk.'

Erika looked pained. 'Could I go?' she offered, spreading her hands in appeal and then recoiling, sick with embarrassment. 'No—of course I can't...' Blinking rapidly to clear the sudden mist from her vision, she made a pretence of folding her coat.

'See you at the pub, then?' The curious hoarseness in Noah's voice spun between them.

'OK.'

'I'll ring when I'm through. Save you hanging about at the pub.'

She nodded, even managing a ragged little smile, just holding back the tears until he'd gone, closing the door quietly behind him.

Erika shoved the last of her textbooks into a carton and taped it closed. That's it, she thought thankfully, lifting it and placing it beside the other items in the hallway.

She glanced at her watch. By the time she'd had a shower and got herself ready Noah should have phoned. She was dreading this goodbye. But I damned well won't cry, she vowed, swallowing the lump in her throat.

Things could have been so different, she thought with a touch of melancholy. But Noah had decided he couldn't trust her word...

She gnawed at her bottom lip. She really did want to get on her way, and hopefully over the border to New South Wales by nightfall. She'd find a motel for the night and then begin the long drive to Melbourne in the morning.

A shower and a change of clothes lifted her spirits somewhat. She fastened the top buttons on her light blue shirt, smoothing the waistband of her jeans and all the time listening for the phone.

What was keeping him? Erika moved to the window yet again and peered out, turning back into the room, willing the phone to ring. And when it did she jumped, her hands unsteady as she picked up the receiver.

'Erika, it's Noah. We're going to have to postpone our drink.'

'But—'

'Just listen,' he rapped. 'Two little kids have gone missing in the bush. I'm about to set out with the search party.'

Erika's heart plummeted. 'Whose kids, Noah?' she questioned sharply, wondering if she knew of them or their parents.

There was an infinitesimal pause, until Noah said heavily, 'Holly—Anne Bryson's little girl.'

'And Isaac?' Erika was already reaching for her car keys.

'Yes, but how did you—?'

'Something Anne once said,' Erika dismissed. 'How long have they been gone?'

'Anne's not sure.' Frustration sounded in Noah's voice. 'She'd taken them on a picnic to Teviot Hills. When they'd eaten, Anne inadvertently fell asleep. When she woke up—the kids had gone. She's blaming herself,' Noah said harshly. 'Saying she wasted valuable time searching and calling.'

Erika felt her throat close. 'Nothing...?'

'No. And the country's steep and scrubby.'

And add to that snakes and ticks and leeches. And heaven knew what else. Erika closed her mind against the terror the two mothers must be feeling. 'What about Issac's mother?' she asked.

'Jacqui—holding together pretty well, actually. Erika—' his voice rose urgently '—they're calling me. I have to go!'

'Noah, wait! I want to help!'

'No!'

'Where are the mothers now?' she demanded, the force of her authority keeping him on the phone.

'At the SES headquarters. But, Erika, you're—'

'I'm there,' she stated, hanging up before he could protest any further.

* * *

Bouncing over the grassy track towards the old hall the State Emergency Service used as their headquarters, Erika marvelled yet again at how quickly the community had responded to this latest emergency.

Already there were assorted vehicles parked around the perimeter. And, please God, she prayed, all this goodwill would translate into a safe and speedy recovery of the children.

Climbing from the car, she ran lightly up the stairs and stopped, her fingers tightening on the handle of her bag. Should she have come? More to the point, would she be welcome? Or had the people of Hillcrest, like Noah, viewed her departure as selfish and shallow? Apprehension began trickling down her spine. Had that been the reason Noah had tried to prevent her from coming here?

Her heart chilled at the thought. She certainly didn't want to embarrass him, or anyone...

'G'day, Doc. Are you coming or going?'

Only gradually did the masculine voice penetrate her senses. 'Rob...' She barely managed a nod.

'Come to help out?' Noah's friend was looking at her with a faintly puzzled expression.

'Um—yes.' She bit her lip.

'Me too,' he said, moving past her into the hall.

Erika blinked, and saw he was carrying a large tray of sandwiches. Suddenly her legs felt like jelly. Nevertheless, she took a deep breath and moved forward into the hall. It was either that or run, she decided, stifling a wild desire to laugh.

The next minutes passed in a mind-numbing blur. And Erika found herself being greeted from all sides. Welcomed.

'Glad you're back, doctor.' Iris Eldridge was busily topping up the tea urns. 'The place wasn't the same without you. Did you enjoy your study leave?'

Study leave? Erika shook her head, as if to clear it. Was that how Noah had explained her absence? And, if it was, did it mean he still cared? The thought warmed her through and through.

CHAPTER TEN

SHE found the mothers of the missing children huddled together on the tubular metal-framed stacking chairs on the far side of the hall.

'Erika...?' Anne looked as though she'd seen a ghost.

'Yes, it's me.' Erika licked her lips. 'I only got back today. I came as soon as I heard.'

Anne nodded, looking dazedly around her. 'This is Jacqui Mitchell, Isaac's mum... Oh, Erika.' Anne began to shake. 'I'll die if anything happens to them.'

'Anne, don't.' Erika took the chair beside the distraught mother. 'Let me give you something.'

'No!' Anne shrank further into the space blanket draped around her shoulders. 'I don't want to be doped out. I want to be here—when they bring Holly b-back.' A sob came up from her boots. 'Dirk said he won't give up until he f-finds her.'

'And if anyone can find the kids, Dirk can.' Jacqui Mitchell spoke for the first time, her voice seeming to have a calming effect on Anne.

'Your little boy is eight, isn't he?' Erika felt drawn by the other's serenity.

'Yes.' Jacqui's mouth moved in a brief smile.

'Then he's bound to be sensible enough to stay

with Holly.' Erika's encouraging words linked the two mothers. 'And they'll be much easier to find if they're together.'

Jacqui lifted a shoulder. 'I'm afraid we can't really predict how Isaac will respond.' She looked directly at Erika. 'My son has Down's Syndrome.'

Erika frowned. Why had no one told her? On the other hand, why should they? Isaac was obviously loved and accepted the way he was.

'Oh, God...' Anne's voice was heart-wrenching.

'Anne...' Erika's voice faltered. 'Show me your hands. What on earth have you done to them?'

Anne's mouth trembled and she looked blankly at her hands as if they belonged to someone else. She shook her head. 'I must have scratched them when I was searching. I tried so hard to find them, Erika...'

'Hush. Of course you did. And they'll be found, Annie. Our men will find them.' Erika hitched up her bag, flipping it open, her hand searching out the bottle of antiseptic spray and a roll of gauze.

Erika made a moue of conjecture. She had no idea what kind of plant-fungi or nettles Anne could have come in contact with. 'When did you last have a tetanus shot, Anne?'

'Noah gave me a jab last year...I made a botch of pruning the roses.'

'You should've worn gloves.' Erika applied the balm of cliché with a smile.

'Or left it to Dirk,' Jacqui said quietly. 'He did offer.'

'I know.' Anne hiccuped a shaky laugh. 'I'll leave everything to him in future.' She looked at her two contemporaries and gave a wobbly smile. 'I'd kill for a cup of tea.'

Providentially, at that moment Iris arrived, with a tray of tea and sandwiches.

'I'll take a cup over to Tom,' Erika offered.

The SES chief was bent over a detailed map of the district. 'How are the lasses bearing up, Doc?' He gave Erika a tight smile.

'Pretty well, really.' Putting the tea down, she stood beside him, her head bent towards the map.

Tom ran a finger around a shaded portion. 'This is roughly where the little ones are lost.'

Erika's heart plummeted. 'It's a big area.' And it was now quite dark. Isaac and Holly would be cold, lonely and so frightened...

'They're all experienced searchers, love.' It was as though Tom Sigley had tapped into her unease. 'And Noah's on hand in case—well, in case of an injury.'

Or worse. Erika bit her lips together, her heart aching for the two mothers. For them the waiting must be agony. Dread increasing by the minute.

Tom took off his reading glasses and placed them carefully on the table. 'If there's no joy tonight, we'll get a chopper up at first light.'

Ten o'clock, and hope which had been high in the early evening had fallen progressively. Rubbing her hands up and down her arms, Erika watched as a new team of searchers was preparing to go out, allowing the first team some respite. Except for Noah and Dirk. Her face tightened. She knew instinctively wild horses wouldn't drag them back until they'd found the children.

She blew out a calming breath. Exhaustion and tension were beginning to catch up with her. She sighed. At least Anne had consented to lie down and was dozing fitfully, but still refusing any kind of sedative.

The ringing of the telephone startled everyone. Picking up the receiver, Tom Sigley asked for hush, but there was no need. An unnatural silence had fallen over the whole place.

He spoke into the mouthpiece, a new haggardness lining his face. 'It's Noah!' he enlightened the assembly.

Erika gripped her hands together, a ring of ice numbing her lips.

And then Tom's hand came up, his fingers splayed in a victory sign. 'They're found! They're OK!'

Making a little moan, Anne struggled out of the makeshift bed. 'I have to get out there.'

The three women went. Anne with Pete Delgado in the front of the ambulance. Erika driving her own car with Jacqui beside her.

And they were there when the search party walked out of the bush, the light from their powerful torches strobing the trees with yellow brilliance.

Erika stood back. This moment was for the mothers and their little ones.

'You waited...?'

She jumped, startled, goosebumps running up and down her spine. It was Noah, barely recognisable under a mask of grime.

Of course she'd waited. Tears of relief were running down her cheeks and she had no idea how painfully tight her arms were around him. 'The kids?' Drawing back, suddenly embarrassed, she scanned his face in the pale moonlight.

'Holly has a sprained ankle.' His mouth folded in on a dry smile. 'Isaac's fine. They'd cuddled up together to keep warm. Smart little kids,' he said, his voice rough with weariness.

The little procession made its way back to the hospital, and when it arrived it was Erika who began issuing orders. 'I'll need Holly Bryson's ankle X-rayed, please,' she said to Helen Dawson, the RN in charge.

Helen blinked. 'Shouldn't you be in America?'

'And miss all the fun?'

'I'll bet Noah was pleased to see you.' Helen sent a laughing look back over her shoulder and began to wheel Holly away for her X-ray.

About as much as he'd like to see a tax collector! Erika sighed, scraping her hair away from the collar of her shirt. She'd seen the guarded look in his eyes before he'd gone off for a shower... And this isn't getting Isaac seen to. Silently taking herself to task, she made her way towards the examination room.

She wiggled her fingers stiffly. She seemed to be cramping up all over. She was dead tired, having given up trying to fathom whether it was night or morning, yesterday or today.

In Sister's office Erika painstakingly rechecked Holly's X-rays, a wistful smile playing about her mouth. Such fine little bones, she marvelled. Thank heaven she was safe. Isaac too. He was the sweetest little boy, full of chat. Erika was glad there'd been no real need to keep either child in hospital and they'd been released into the care of their respective mothers.

Folding her hands in front of her, she stared into space. She should have been miles away by now, the pain of parting behind her. Except it wouldn't really be behind her. She'd carry it around in her heart for a long time to come...

'You should be home in bed.' Noah's words cut across her thoughts and she blinked up at him. He was watching her, the expression in his eyes masked by the shadows cast by the lamp between them.

Erika tried to smile, but her mouth got all out of shape in a jumble of emotions. And he was so close she could smell the clean soap-and-water freshness on his skin.

'You look like hell,' he said bluntly.

She brought her chin up. 'Fancy that.'

Noah's mouth crimped around a smile. 'Come on.' He put out a hand towards her. 'Let's get you home.'

But where was *home* any more? Outside the air was clear and sharp. Erika felt a slight dizziness overtake her, the ground coming up to meet her. 'Oh—'

'You're out on your feet,' Noah growled, wrapping a supporting arm around her shoulders. 'When did you fly in?'

'This morning,' she mumbled, wondering why her eyelids felt weighted down. 'Direct from LA. What about my car?' she insisted, when they stopped at his Land Rover.

'You can collect it tomorrow.' He swung open the passenger door, scooped her up and lifted her in.

'It's tomorrow already...' Erika muffled the words in his dark bulk as he settled in beside her.

His gaze flickered for a moment. 'Don't you know tomorrow never comes?' He turned his head, waiting for her answer, but she was already asleep.

Erika woke to silence and the gentlest breeze wafting through the partly open window. Blinking uncertainly, she half raised her head and then she remembered...

She muffled a groan into the pillow. Noah must have got her to bed when he'd driven her home from the hospital. What else had he done? Cautiously, she put a hand under the duvet and touched her jeans. Thank heavens. Except for her shoes, he hadn't attempted to undress her. Nevertheless, the whole scenario sent a wave of vulnerability right through her.

The sharp click of the front door closing had her sitting boldly upright, pulling her knees up to her chin. 'Noah...?' Her voice came out on a croak. 'Is that you?'

'Ah...' Noah's dark head came round the door. 'Sleeping Beauty's awake, I see.'

Erika blushed, watching him amble into the bedroom, his powerful masculinity making the space appear to shrink to the size of a doll's house. 'Good sleep?' he asked.

'It was,' she confessed ruefully. 'What time is it?'

'Five-ish.'

Erika frowned. 'Five-ish when?'

'Sunday afternoon.'

'You mean to tell me I've slept almost fifteen hours?' Agitatedly, she ran her fingers through her hair, locking them on top of her head.

He looked at her with steady eyes. 'Jet-lag will do that to you every time. I've just come from Peaches.' He held up the carrier bag he was toting. 'Marianne's sent along some minestrone and home-made bread. Hungry?'

'Starving.' She smiled a bit uncertainly, her heart beating harder at the prospect of sharing a meal with him after so long. 'But at the moment I need the bathroom more than I need food.'

A wry smile nipped his mouth. 'See you in a bit, then. Oh, by the way.' He dropped her keys on the bedside table. 'I've brought your car back.'

Erika waited until he'd gone, then she slid out of bed, her eyes suddenly registering the presence of her small suitcase neatly placed against the wall. She bit her lip. Noah must have brought it in from the boot of her car.

What did it all mean? The feeling of apprehension rushed at her again, and she tried to identify the shapeless thoughts invading her jet-lagged brain.

Was she being lulled into a false sense of security? Did Noah's actions mean anything more than just plain good manners?

Her heart did a U-turn. He'd brought the food, anticipated she'd need her suitcase. Surely it added up to someone caring. It certainly didn't appear like the actions of someone about to run her out of town.

Air whistled out of her lungs, ending in an explosive little sigh. Conjecture was getting her nowhere. Hefting the suitcase on to the bed, she opened it and took out fresh underclothes and her cotton robe, then made her way to the bathroom.

It was only after she'd showered and towelled herself dry Erika noticed a misty rain was falling. Nice for the farmers' crops, she thought absently, pulling a brush through her hair.

She left her face unadorned, an odd flutter of shyness assailing her as she left the bedroom and made her way along the short length of the hallway to the kitchen.

Noah had set places at the tables. She stood for a moment and watched him, her eyes lingering, drinking in his maleness. He was wearing a black T-shirt that delineated the tight group of muscles beneath and a pair of jeans that were clean but had definitely seen better days.

'Something smells good,' she said, unable to stop her smile as he turned quickly and caught her watching him.

'Just making sure the minestrone's nice and hot.' He sent her a youthful, lopsided grin, eyeing her sleek black leggings and pearl-grey top. 'Feeling better?'

'Much.' She joined him at the stove. 'Anything I can do to help?'

He turned off the heat and gave the minestrone a final stir. 'Couple of bowls might be a good idea. Then we'll be in business.'

'Another?' Noah's look was softly indulgent as Erika neared the end of her second bowl of soup.

'Heavens, no!' She gave a shaky laugh. 'But that was out of this world—delicious!'

'When did you last eat?' he asked.

She paused, thinking. 'I had a sandwich at the hall last night.'

Noah rolled his eyes. 'I meant when did you last have a proper meal?'

She lifted a shoulder. 'I had some kind of curry on the plane.'

'That would have been on Friday evening our time.' His dark brows drew together. 'It must have been some kind of miracle you stayed on your feet as long as you did,' he persisted in a low tone. 'The folk of Hillcrest are very grateful.'

'For what?' She looked startled.

'For showing the flag when you must have been dog-tired. Keeping everyone's spirits up. Looking after Anne and Jacqui, plus the children when they were found.'

'That's crazy.' She shook her head. 'It wasn't just me.'

'But you're the doctor.' His mouth compressed for a second. 'That title means something in a rural community.'

She paused, biting her lip. 'I let you down, didn't I? Just up and leaving like that?'

He grimaced. 'Perhaps we let each other down. I acted like a clod—especially yesterday at the surgery. I'm sorry.'

She met his eyes and found them somewhat guarded. 'You created a kind of cover story for me, didn't you?'

He shifted awkwardly. 'Seeing I practically told you to leave and not bother coming back, it seemed the least I could do. And when I was asked directly I said you were on extended study leave.' His eyes burned with a strange intensity. 'All I wanted to do was to stop idle conjecture about your leaving.'

Thus allowing their credibility as a medical team to remain intact. That was if it was going to matter anyway. She was gathering no indication of what Noah was really feeling. Nevertheless... 'You didn't have to do that,' she said softly. 'But thank you anyway.'

He gave a taut smile. 'We should've talked. I shouldn't have let you go like that. It was a crummy way to end your locum tenure.'

He looked at her then, a tiny pulse beating in his throat, an erratic flutter that Erika knew was being echoed in her own body. 'I meant to prepare you,' she said. 'But in the end there was no time. In hindsight, I think I acted rather selfishly.'

'Well, it's water under the bridge now.' Standing to his feet, he collected their used dishes, taking them across to the sink as though putting an end to further discussion.

Watching him, his quick, purposeful manner, Erika felt dismissed. But not for long. Her lips tightening, she rose from the table, moving across to join him at the window, peering out. 'It's raining in earnest now.'

'Mmm.' Noah's heart was beating like a tom-tom. Lord, how he'd missed her! And now she was back, barely centimetres away from him, her faint, delicate fragrance teasing his senses, making a mockery of his control. Damn! There was so much he wanted to say to her, but for the life of him he couldn't seem to get his tongue to co-operate.

'Noah?'

He blinked and turned his head a fraction. Her eyes were cast down, her long gold-tipped lashes fanning across her cheeks. He spoke in a rush. 'What about some coffee?'

'No—at least not yet.' She swallowed convulsively. 'Is there still a place here for me?'

He shrugged. 'I rather think the townspeople would lynch me if I let you leave now.'

Her gaze faltered. 'What about you, though? Do you still want me here?'

There was a breathless little silence, and Erika felt sure that if a pin had dropped she would have heard it. So much depended on what he told her now. So much. Probably what she did with the rest of her life.

'Erika—' he began to speak and then broke off as his mobile phone shrilled its summons.

Erika turned away, feeling an unkind fate had stepped in again, the result leaving her feeling more vulnerable than ever.

'I'll have to go.' Noah closed the phone with a snap and pocketed it.

'What is it?' Erika's professional instincts flew into overdrive.

'A young couple have just arrived at the hospital.' Noah pushed his hands through his hair. 'The woman's in labour. Anne says she's nearly full-term but very slight of build. She may need help to deliver. I'll need your car, Erika.'

'I'm coming with you.' Without giving him time to argue, she dashed into her bedroom, collecting her keys and a wind-jacket. 'Here, catch.' She tossed the set of keys to Noah, and together they ran out into the pouring rain.

Erika felt her nerves screw tight, her gaze following the urgent rhythm of the windscreen wipers as they slicked against the force of the rain. 'Surely Anne isn't fit to be at work today?' With a flick of her head she turned questioningly to Noah.

'Normal rules don't apply in isolated areas of medicine, Erika,' he said bluntly.

'I'm aware of that. But Anne's been under a terrible strain over the past twenty-four hours.'

'Well, the hospital doesn't have the luxury of a list of on-call nurses they can fall back on. Anne was probably rostered, so she had no alternative but to come to work.' He tossed Erika a dry look. 'Just be thankful she's on duty. At least she's had some midwifery training.'

Erika's hands clenched as Noah took the climb to the hospital. She beat back a feeling of unease. It was like flying blind, she thought. They had no idea what was waiting for them at the hospital. What possible problems the young woman's labour might present them with. And they had no humidicrib...

Anne met them at the nurses' station. 'Oh, good. You've both come,' she said, as if seeing them together was no great surprise.

'What can you tell us, Annie?' Noah's voice was clipped.

'Our couple are Todd and Sally Everett. They're

very young, and by the look of them scared to death about what's happening.'

'They damned well ought to be,' Noah muttered. 'What if they'd been caught in a real emergency? Were they intending to deliver the baby on the side of the road?'

'Noah—' Erika placed a cautionary hand on his arm. 'They're here now. That's all that counts.'

'I've put Sally straight into the delivery room.' Anne led the way along the short corridor. 'But I've alerted Pete Delgado. Just in case there's still time to send her on to Warwick.'

One look at their patient told both doctors this was not going to happen. Whatever their misgivings, Sally was going to have her baby in Hillcrest Hospital. Under their gentle questioning she revealed her labour had progressed slowly and steadily all day.

'We've been on the road for most of the day. I've come here to try to find a job.' Todd Everett held tightly on to his wife's hand. 'Sal started to feel sick so we had to find a hospital fast.'

'Right.' Noah's tone was brisk. He turned to the young man. 'We'll need to examine Sally now, so if you'd step outside for a few minutes?'

At the door Todd turned, casting a lingering look at his wife. 'I won't be far away, Sal.'

'She's tiny, isn't she?' Erika murmured as they scrubbed.

'Mmm.' Noah chewed his lip thoughtfully. 'She might be in for a bumpy ride.'

Erika sent him a quick discerning look, knowing the possibility of a Caesarean section was uppermost in their minds.

'Let's hope not.' Noah pulled on his gloves and, turning, sent a reassuring smile across to Sally. 'I'll be as gentle as I can, Sally,' he said, beginning his internal examination.

Sally looked numbly at him with huge, frightened eyes.

'She's fully dilated and the baby seems small.' Noah quietly gave his findings to Erika. 'I'd be inclined to let her try to deliver naturally. Let's get an IV in as a precaution, shall we? Normal saline.'

Erika nodded, moving swiftly to cannulate Sally. The fluids would keep the line open, saving them precious time in the event of an emergency, when drugs would have to be injected stat. She felt a surge of energy. It was going to take their combined skills, but she was sure even with their lack of equipment they could deliver Sally of a healthy baby.

But thirty minutes later she wasn't so sure. Each contraction seemed longer and more painful than the last and Sally was becoming distressed.

Standing at his wife's head, Todd swore, looking accusingly at the doctors. 'Can't you do something for her?'

'We can't give her any painkillers.' Noah was firm. 'Sally's progressed too far into her labour. Any drugs now would cross the placenta and harm your baby. Come on, now, Sally,' he coaxed. 'You're nearly there. You can do it.'

'I can't!' she wailed. 'Todd—help me—'

Todd's thin arms gripped his wife's shoulders. 'I would if I could, Sal.' He bent, sending wild kisses across the top of her head. 'You have to do it, honey. You have to get our baby born.'

'How's her blood pressure, Anne?' Noah's face was set in harsh lines.

Anne took the reading. 'One-sixty over seventy.'

Erika pressed her lips together. The BP was elevated, but that was to be expected. Sally was probably experiencing the equivalent of running a very hard race. A flutter of unease filtered through her. Had they done the right thing in allowing this petite girl to try for a natural birth? She looked so brittle she could break in two. Erika moved swiftly. The only safe measure left to them now was for Sally to use the nitrous oxide gas.

Quickly she unhooked the mask from its stand and instructed Sally how to use it, praying the gas would blur the pain and help Sally ride out the contractions.

'Heart rate one-eighty,' Anne said calmly.

'Come on, Sally...' Noah was cajoling. 'Here's a big one. Give me a push. And again. Don't strain—good work. You're nearly there.' He spun to Anne. 'Episiotomy tray ready?'

'Hold off, Noah,' Erika cut in urgently. 'She may not tear. No, she won't.' Erika's voice held pure relief as the baby's head crowned. 'Well done, Sally!'

'You have a daughter,' Noah said, expertly clamping and cutting the cord. In seconds he'd removed the infant to a nearby examination table.

One glance at the newborn's stillness, her blueness, told Erika they had a problem. Her heart squeezed up with apprehension.

His face grim, Noah ran his stethoscope over the infant. 'We've got a heartbeat,' he gritted, tossing his stethoscope to one side. 'I'll suction. Get ready to bag her, Erika. We're not losing this little sweetheart.'

With no time to waste, Erika placed the tiny airviva mask over the baby's nose and mouth. Come *on*, she pleaded silently, willing her own breath into the flat little lungs. Within seconds there was a sound between a splutter and a cough, followed by an angry little squawk. Thank God. Her eyes met Noah's.

He nodded, his mouth compressing. 'She'll make it.'

'Yes.' Erika's legs felt like jelly.

'I'd like her on hundred per cent oxygen.' He removed his gloves with a savage yank. 'Monitor five-minutely for the next thirty minutes. I'll leave you to do her check.' Turning, he shouldered his way through the door, ripping off his gown as he went.

Anne's raised eyebrow spoke volumes.

Erika blinked, feeling tears of reaction clogging

her throat. She had more than a fair idea why Noah had left so abruptly. Deftly, she inserted the baby's tiny nasal tube, leaving Anne to swaddle the newborn little girl.

Thirty minutes later, with Sally tidied up and the baby checked over, Erika left the new parents clucking happily over their daughter and went to find Noah.

CHAPTER ELEVEN

SHE found him in the hospital kitchen. He was sitting at the table, seemingly staring into space, his hands clamped around a large tea mug.

Erika's heart leapt anew at the sight of him. It was crazy, she thought. She'd seen him just minutes ago.

Shaken, she tested the tea for freshness and proceeded to pour herself a cup. Would it always be like this? she wondered. If she had no alternative than to leave Hillcrest, would she have him in her heart and in her head for the rest of her life?

Noah lifted his head and smiled briefly at her. 'Baby OK?'

'She's lovely.' Erika pulled out a chair and sat opposite him. 'Todd and Sally are delighted with her. They're naming her Caitlin.'

'Sweet.' Noah drained his tea. 'Do you think they have any idea how very fortunate they've been?'

Erika's mouth turned down. 'Probably not.'

'It could have been a whole different story, couldn't it?' Noah frowned into his empty mug. 'If the baby had been premature?'

'Don't.' Erika suppressed a shiver.

His forefinger traced the rim of his mug. 'I've

been sitting here contemplating the idea of closing down the entire midwifery service. Letting it be known that in future any expectant mothers will have to make alternative arrangements about where to have their babies.'

Erika frowned. She'd sensed in the delivery room he'd been nearing the end of his tether. And it was understandable. Working a large practice on his own as he'd been doing must at some time take its toll. And, after being up half the night searching for the lost children, the drama with the Everetts had more than likely been the last straw.

'That would be a terrible shame,' she said carefully. 'And would it really achieve your peace of mind in the long term? Whether you like it or not, Noah, there'll always be another emergency—next week, next month.'

'Tell me about it!' He spanned his temple, massaging an obvious ache. 'I'm just fed up with being put through the wringer by stupid, thoughtless people who don't give a damn about the hardships we face.'

Erika cupped her chin on her hand and looked earnestly at him. 'Don't beat up on yourself, Noah. Your professional judgement is impeccable.' She moued wryly. 'But I agree today with Sally was a bit iffy.'

She ignored his outraged snort and continued.

'As I see it, even as isolated as you are, wouldn't it be better to have a limited maternity facility than none at all?

'And the Everetts aren't stupid,' she reproved softly. 'A bit thoughtless, perhaps. And young. But they're a family now.' She smiled a bit tentatively. 'If you could have seen their faces when they could at last hold their baby—well, it was all the reward I needed, knowing I'd had a hand in bringing about such a happy outcome.'

'Good grief,' Noah said faintly.

'What?' She huffed a cracked laugh.

'You're amazing.'

She blushed.

'There is an alternative, of course.' A smile began deep in his eyes and tilted his mouth.

'There is?'

'Mmm.' Standing, he collected their tea mugs and took them across to the dishwasher. 'You could get busy organising your Italian festival. Make us some money so we can get a humidicrib and a dozen other things for the comfort of our birthing mums.'

Erika's mouth dried. Was he saying what she thought he was saying? And if he was... A dulled resentment boiled over, fuelled by her anxiety about where she actually stood with him, her uncertain future. Slowly she stood to her feet. 'Ask me properly, then.'

He shot her a loaded look before closing the dishwasher. 'I'll need you up close for that.'

'Oh, you—' With a low curl of laughter, she ran to him, feeling the breath almost knocked out of her as he gathered her in.

As though drawn by magnets, their lips met, the passion rocking them to the core.

'Stay, Erika,' he said hoarsely, smoothing the back of her hair with his hand. 'I need you. I love you. You're the absolute in my life, the blue in my sky.'

'Oh, Noah.' She swallowed, blinking back the tears of joy. 'What lovely things to say.' Lifting her hands, she bracketed his face. 'I love you too,' she said breathily. 'I thought you wanted me to leave—'

'Never.' His mouth came down hungrily. Then he raised his head and swore softly. 'This is a hell of a place to be doing this.'

'Oh, I don't know...' The tip of her finger outlined his mouth.

'You've shocked me, Dr Somers.' His eyes went speculatively around the room and then he grinned. 'I wonder...'

'Noah!' She gave a protesting squeal as he lifted her right off her feet. 'Stop! Noah! I was kidding!'

'But not about loving me?' He placed her feet firmly back on the floor.

'No.' A solemn light came into her eyes. 'Not about that.'

He took her face in his hands, gazing deeply into her eyes. 'This is for keeps, you know.'

Her breath caught. 'Is this a marriage proposal, Dr Jameson?'

He laughed, dropping a kiss on her mouth. 'The townsfolk would be disapproving of anything else.'

'We've lots of plans to make, then.' Her voice was dreamy.

'Tomorrow,' he said. 'Right now, this guy just wants to take his girl home.'

'We'll phone our respective families tomorrow,' Noah said, as they drove through the rainy night.

'Mmm.' Erika smiled contentedly and rested her head against his shoulder. 'And, just to keep things official, I guess I'd better sign a partnership agreement.'

'Not a problem,' he said, reaching out and capturing her hand completely. 'You can sign *the* partnership agreement. It's still locked away in my desk.'

'How smug!' She rounded a laughing gaze on him. 'You always knew I'd come back, didn't you?'

'Let's say I hoped.' He touched her fingers to his mouth. 'Happy?'

She snuggled closer. 'Happy' didn't even begin to describe it.

There was no awkwardness between them when they got back to her flat. Without haste, they went into her bedroom, and in the silvered light from the bedlamp they undressed each other.

'Oh...' Erika turned and put a hand to her mouth. 'I forgot I hadn't made the bed.'

'We'd only have to unmake it,' Noah growled, scooping her up and laying her gently down.

'You're so beautiful,' he murmured, coming to lie on the bed beside her. 'I'm wild for you, Erika.'

'That's how you told me it should be...' Her voice trailed off and she found it hard to speak.

'And wasn't I right?' His breathing quickened, a flush deepening along his cheekbones.

'Yes. Oh, yes...'

They kissed fiercely, deeply. And this is what it's all about, she marvelled, as excitement and the most incredible joy tumbled through her blood.

And then it was Noah's body and hers in a dance as old as time, matching, sharing. And she felt so special, so loved, her spirit soaring to meet his, crowning, complete in the greatest gift of all.

Several days later Erika knocked on the door of Noah's consulting room and popped her head in. 'Is this a good time for a staff meeting?'

'Ah, Dr Somers.' Noah looked up and sent her a lazy grin. 'Come on in.'

'It's such a lovely day.' Erika closed the door behind her and stood against it. 'I thought we could sit out on the back verandah. And I've asked Jenny to join us for a coffee break.'

He rolled his eyes in resignation and Erika sent him a reproving look.

'We've hardly had a minute to talk with her since we announced our engagement,' she justified.

'I know.' Noah got slowly to his feet. 'And I'll just bet our Jen is bursting with questions.'

'Something like that.' With a small grin, Erika

tucked herself in against him. 'Did you sleep well?'

'Oh, love...' Noah brushed the backs of his fingers over her cheeks. 'Need you ask?'

She turned her face up to his. 'I want to discuss the Everetts.'

He kissed her very softly, very possessively. 'I'd rather discuss us.'

'And we shall.' She gave a shaky laugh, tugging him towards the door. 'After we've dealt with Jenny and the Everetts.'

It was obvious Jenny could hardly contain her curiosity, and when they were settled over coffee and apple sponge, she asked bluntly, 'Well, you two, when's the wedding?'

Noah's eyes glinted briefly. 'All in good time, Jen. For the moment we're just enjoying being engaged.'

Jenny sniffed. 'Well, the least you could do, Noah, is buy the girl a ring!'

He looked affronted. 'It's all in hand. We're having it made. And the wedding rings to match.'

'Oh, how romantic!' Jenny's face lit up. 'And where will you be married? Our little St Bede's has just been refurbished, you know.'

Noah exchanged a helpless look with Erika. 'It's usual for the wedding to take place in the bride's parish, Jen.'

'Oh—how silly of me.' Jenny coloured faintly. 'Making wild assumptions—'

'No, you haven't,' Erika came in gently. 'It's

just that my parents will have people they'll want to invite, and anywhere other than Melbourne would be impractical.'

'Of course it would.' Jenny was brisk. 'But at least let me know the date in plenty of time.' She smiled. 'A group of us want to give you a bridal shower.'

'Oh, Jen...' Erika was deeply touched. 'Thank you. I never expected—' She bit her lip. 'And I will let you know,' she promised. 'Just as soon as we fix a date.'

'We'll have it at my house.' Jenny had recovered her poise completely. 'And you, young man—' she looked pointedly at Noah '—get your skates on. It still takes a while to obtain a marriage licence, you know.'

'She's such a mother hen,' Erika said indulgently, when Jenny had departed inside. 'And fancy them wanting to give me a shower.'

Noah lifted a shoulder. 'Just bears out what I've been telling you. The whole place has taken you to their hearts.' He reached out and took her hands, his gaze softly questioning. 'Just where *are* we getting married anyway? Do you have somewhere in mind?'

Her eyes went misty. 'My old school chapel— if that's all right with you?'

'Anywhere is all right with me.' He touched a kiss to the curve of her throat. 'Even under a gum tree would suit me just fine.'

She shook her head.

'Not a good idea?'

'No. My parents would never forgive me.'

He eyed her thoughtfully for a moment. 'Are they pleased, do you think?'

'Of course they're pleased. You spoke to them both, Noah. Did you get a different impression?'

His mouth flattened. 'Well, at least your mother sounded charming.'

Erika sent him a dry look. 'Dad will thaw. Just give him a bit of time.' She chuckled. 'Besides, you called him *sir*. That would have pleased him no end.'

Noah snorted. 'I could hardly call him *Ewen*!'

'You will be by the time we get married,' she predicted confidently. 'Now, come on, Doctor.' She touched a swirl of his hair. 'The world hasn't stopped just because we're getting married. What are we doing about the Everetts?'

Noah finished his coffee in a gulp. 'How is Sally doing?'

'Bounced back extremely well. And the baby's feeding nicely. I can't in conscience keep them much longer. But on the other hand…' She made a small moue. 'A caravan park is not exactly where I'd choose to see them go either.'

'Maybe it won't come to that.' Consideringly, Noah scraped a hand across his cheekbones. 'By sheer coincidence, I was speaking to Michael Petani yesterday. Apparently, he's now in a position to employ someone part-time.'

'Oh, good.' Erika looked pleased. 'That will relieve Tara. But how does it affect the Everetts?'

'I'm coming to that.' Noah looked at her measuredly. 'It seems there's a cottage available with the job. Michael and Tara lived there when they were first married. They've since moved on up to the family home now Michael's parents have retired to town.'

'So, what are you saying?' Erika propped her chin on her hand and looked questioningly at him.

'I told Michael about Todd looking for work. He seemed interested. In fact...' Noah glanced at his watch. 'They should be meeting about now.'

Erika chewed her lip thoughtfully. 'But would a part-time job be enough for the Everetts to live on?'

'Well, the cottage is rent-free,' Noah pointed out. 'And they'd have fresh eggs and farm produce thrown in.'

'And Anne's already given Sally a huge pile of Holly's baby clothes.'

'There you are, then,' Noah said as they exchanged a grin. 'And Michael said if the farm continues to do well the job could go to full-time.'

'What a lovely, positive outcome.' Erika sighed with satisfaction.

'Let's just hope the young men will take to one another.' Noah sounded a note of caution.

'They will.' Erika's smile was ringed with confidence. They stood up from their chairs. 'And the girls will be company for each other too. And the babies—' She broke off and bit her lip. 'What?'

'You.' His eyes caressed her tenderly. 'I love you, Erika.'

Her breath caught. 'And I love you, Noah.'

'Keep telling me.' He touched his mouth to hers. 'I have a shocking memory.'

'You don't,' she reproved, nudging her forehead against his. 'You just like to look helpless.'

'Helpless? Me?' He gave a smothered snort of laughter. 'I'll show you *helpless*, Doctor!'

'Noah—stop!' Erika gave a stifled yelp as he lifted her bodily. 'Behave—' Her protest came to an abrupt halt as their lips met and clung.

'Let's get married soon?' Gaze intent, Noah set her down. With gentle fingers he spread her hair away from her face. 'Could you make a list of things we have to do?'

She nodded, recognising the little spiral in her tummy as pure, unadulterated happiness.

'We'll fly to Brisbane next weekend,' he decided. 'You can meet my family.'

'And collect our rings from the jeweller,' she whispered, curling herself in against him, drawing his face down to hers.

'That's looking very good, Mr Eldridge.' Erika placed her stethoscope to one side and made a final note on Clem Eldridge's file. Looking up, she smiled at the elderly man. 'How was the holiday?'

'Well, to tell you the truth, Doctor—' Clem

measured his words carefully '—I actually enjoyed meself. Never thought I would—Sydney being such a big place and that. But me and Iris pottered about, saw things we never thought to see. Yes.' He considered, painstakingly fastening his shirt buttons. 'It was a darn good holiday.'

'That's wonderful.' Erika held back a smile, guessing Clem had probably never been so voluble in his entire life. 'Don't forget to have your script filled, will you?' Standing quickly, she walked him to the door.

Clem tapped his shirt pocket. 'I won't.'

'Oh, and remind Iris the exercise class begins in a couple of weeks. It's especially for seniors, so she may like to come along.'

Clem nodded. 'She'll be there. Iris wouldn't miss something like that.' He put a gentle hand on Erika's arm. 'All the best for your big day, lass. You and Noah will have a grand marriage. And it's not just me and Iris reckon that.'

Blindly, Erika went back to her desk and sat there. The endless goodwill of this small community had literally stunned her. Was still stunning her.

'Oh, Lord,' she whispered. She felt suddenly emotional. Like bawling her eyes out. Blinking fast, she set her lips, taking up her pen and hooking her diary open. It was time she and Noah made some firm plans. Applied for a marriage licence and set a wedding date.

Her head came up at the soft knock on her door, and then it opened and Noah came in.

'Hello,' she said softly, gripped by a blinding pleasure at just seeing him standing there. Springing up from her chair, she ran to him, sliding her arms around him. 'I've never been so happy,' she said shakily, pressing kisses all over his face and stroking the little tufts of hair away from his temple.

'Oh, sweet...' Noah's hands kneaded her spine gently. 'It's time we were married.'

'That's just what I was thinking.' She sent him a dazzling smile. 'When? Let's make a date now.'

'Erika...' Noah held her away and look intently into her eyes. 'One thing at a time.'

'Oh...' She looked uncertain. 'You seem so serious. Has the bank foreclosed on our mortgage?'

'No.' He huffed a dry laugh. 'But your father's here.'

'Here?' Her eyes rounded in disbelief.

'Twenty minutes ago.' Noah took a step backwards, shovelling his hands through his hair. 'He's sitting in my surgery now.'

'Oh, darling.' Erika bit her lip. 'Did he give you a hard time?'

Noah's look was rueful. 'Well, he didn't beat about the bush. Certainly asked all the questions a prospective father-in-law might ask.'

'Did you mind?' Erika went to him again, winding her arms around his neck. 'That's just Dad's way.'

Noah's smile was strained. 'As long as he doesn't try to talk you out of marrying me. He didn't mince words about his hopes you'd specialise one day. Perhaps he imagines I'm the GP clod who's holding you back?'

Erika looked shocked. 'Bite your tongue, Doctor. You're my life, you crazy man. I want to marry you, have babies with you. Grow old together. And, sure, I may specialise. Some day. But it will be because I want to and not because my father thinks I ought.'

'Oh, God, I needed to hear you say that.' Noah put his arms around her, burying his face in her hair, holding her so tightly she could hardly breathe.

'Sweetheart...' Erika tipped her head back and kissed him gently. 'We're getting married.'

'Yes.' He took a deep breath.

Erika's eyes narrowed in speculation. 'Did Dad say whether Mum came with him?'

'She's over at the motel, apparently.' Noah gave her a long look. 'Your father said they'd decided on the spur of the moment to have a motoring holiday in Queensland. Thought they'd stop off and see us.'

'Sly old fox.' Erika spun away towards the window. 'But I'll beat him at his own game yet.'

Noah looked baffled. He waited a minute, then joined her at the window, winding an arm around her shoulders. 'I know that look, Erika,' he said. 'What are you up to?'

'Just thinking.' Her eyes feasted on the outside. The light of early afternoon lay on the verandah like golden swatches spiked with the shifting patterns of the treeferns and eucalypts. And there was the soft drone of a tractor, the click of a cicada in the shrubbery under the window. Lifting her head, she turned and manoeuvred herself in against him. 'What would you say to getting married in the next few days? Here.'

'Here?' Noah frowned. 'But I thought you wanted your old school chapel?'

'Oh, that!' She lifted a shoulder dismissively. 'It all seems so simple,' she said, fiddling with the buttons on his shirt. 'My parents are already here. And your family could get here at short notice, couldn't they?'

He grinned, stroking the hair back behind her ear. 'It's only a matter of getting a flight. I've already asked Paul to be my best man.'

'And I'll ask Anne to be my matron of honour.' Erika was thinking quickly. 'And Holly could be a part of our wedding. Flower girl, perhaps? Or should I have Dakota?' She looked at Noah after a slight hesitation.

He shook his head. 'She's a bit young, and Kim's got enough on her plate without organising that.'

'You're right.' She tapped a finger to her lips. 'I'm sure Dean and Jas could take a couple of days off to be here. Matthew's in London, so he's out. Oh, well, that can't be helped.'

'Erika?' He slid both hands up her throat and cupped her face. 'You're not making all these changes for my sake, are you? I mean, you seemed so set on Melbourne and pleasing your parents—'

'No,' she cut in huskily. 'Let me tell you why it's right for us to be married here.'

'Go on.' He ran his fingers up the back of her neck, gently twisting them in her hair.

'It just kind of hit me,' she said, unable to tear her eyes away from his. She fluttered a hand towards the open window. 'Melbourne isn't home for me any more. Home really isn't a place at all, is it? It's people. Our people of Hillcrest.' She stared into his eyes, so blue and steady. 'We'll have a lovely wedding.'

Noah bent his head and kissed her lips. 'What about a week from today? That would make it next Saturday.'

'Perfect.' Her face was suddenly alive with purpose. She looked at her watch. 'I've finished my list. Have you?' When he nodded, she said happily, 'Then we'd better get ourselves over to St Bede's. See if Father Corelli can do us a wedding at short notice.'

'Damn!' Noah suddenly clapped a hand to his head. 'We don't have a marriage licence.'

Erika looked stricken, and then her lips twitched. 'Not a problem, Doctor. Don't you realise my father is an expert at pulling strings? Come on.' She tugged him towards the door. 'I'm dying to see his face when we tell him our plans.'

* * *

Next day, Erika went into a huddle with Anne.

'I'm so thrilled you've asked me to be a part of your wedding,' Anne said. 'But honestly, Erika, I don't have a thing I could wear. It's years since I had a posh dress. And Holly's wardrobe is practically all jeans and T-shirts.'

'Stop fretting, Annie.' Erika topped up their wine glasses. 'I thought we could take Tuesday afternoon off and go across to Warwick. Shop till we drop.'

'But what about your own dress?' Anne looked thoughtful. 'One afternoon mightn't be enough time to find something you really like.'

'I already have my dress.' Erika gave a mysterious half-smile. 'I bought it in the States. An exclusive.'

Anne's eyes popped. 'You're wearing a designer wedding dress?'

Erika gave a throaty chuckle. 'Well, let's just say it's more a dress for a wedding. But I will need shoes,' she said. 'And we're not to worry about the expense either. My dad's picking up the tab for the entire wedding.' Erika's laugh tinkled. 'He's on quite a roll. Anyone would think he'd suggested us having the wedding here himself.'

'I actually met him this morning.' Anne took a mouthful of her wine. 'When Noah was showing him over the hospital. He was charming.'

Erika's last patient on Friday afternoon was Jacob Petani.

'I feel the slackest mother on earth.' Tara's mouth turned down comically. 'Jacob was due for his first lot of shots a couple of weeks ago. It was Sally who reminded me.'

'You and she getting on OK, then?' Erika tossed over her shoulder as she prepared the immunisation cocktail.

'Oh, yes. She's sweet. And she's got the cottage looking great. Do you want Jake on the bed?' she asked, as Erika returned with the injection.

'No, just hold him.' Erika smiled. 'That's lovely.'

'I hope he doesn't cry.' Tara held her son tightly. 'There, baby,' she crooned, as Erika swabbed and made the job swiftly. 'All over now.' Jacob's bottom lip wobbled and he gave an offended little sob. 'Oh, sweetheart. Come on now.' Expertly, she lifted her T-shirt and tucked him on to her breast.

Erika chuckled. 'Comfort zone, hmm?'

'For both of us, I think.' Tara looked down at her son as he suckled noisily.

'He's gorgeous, Tara.' Erika's look was rapt. 'And hasn't he grown?'

Tara grinned. 'You and Noah planning to have one of these yourselves, by any chance?'

'Hope so.' Erika coloured prettily. 'And sooner rather than later.'

'Terrific.' Jacob had fallen instantly asleep, and Tara eased him away from her nipple. 'Are you getting a honeymoon?'

'Just Saturday night and Sunday.' Erika capped her pen and placed the Petani family file to one side. 'But that's all right. We'll probably organise some time off later in the year. Want me to hold him for a tick?'

'Thanks, Erika.' Tara adjusted her clothes and then took her son back, carefully cradling him in the crook of her arm. 'And thanks for squeezing us in this afternoon.'

'You're welcome.' Erika touched a finger to Jacob's soft thatch of dark hair. 'Oh, take this record card to remind you when his next shot's due.'

'Thanks.' Tara tucked it in the pocket of her jeans. At the door she turned and grinned. 'See you tomorrow, then?'

'Tomorrow?' Erika blinked.

Tara rolled her eyes, looking both indulgent and exasperated. 'At the wedding!'

'Oh—of course!' Erika clapped the back of her hand against her mouth to stifle a giggle. 'I'll be there.'

CHAPTER TWELVE

THE wedding was lovely, the little church of St Bede's packed with well-wishers.

Anne had arrived in plenty of time to help Erika get ready. 'Like it?' Anne spun around, showing off her own finery, a slimline silk concoction in softest gold.

'You look fabulous, Anne.' Erika smiled in satisfaction. 'Told you the colour was right.'

Anne giggled. 'I've never owned anything so grand in my life. Your mum joining us?'

'In a while.' Erika inspected her silk stockings with a critical eye. 'She's over at Peaches doing the place-cards for the reception. With Jenny's help, of course.'

They exchanged a good-natured chuckle.

'And Holly's dressed and waiting,' Anne said. 'Almost sick with excitement, poor baby. Jacqui's going to drop her off here a bit later.'

Erika gave a shaky laugh. 'I feel a bit sick myself, actually. What about a glass of wine, Annie?'

'Coming up.' Annie smiled understandingly. 'Although probably we should be good girls and have a cup of tea instead. But what the heck! You're getting married!'

Erika's hair and make-up were done and Iris had

delivered their flowers, simple but beautiful posies of roses, stephanotis and baby's breath.

'Oh, they're just what I wanted,' Erika sighed, touching the trail of pale ribbons.

'Our Iris definitely has a way with flowers,' Anne agreed. 'Ready for your dress now?' Almost reverently, she slipped the cream silk-satin gown off its hanger and held it ready for Erika to step into.

She did so, slowly and carefully, standing perfectly still while Anne deftly slid the zipper home.

'Well, what do you think, Anne? OK?' Erika twirled this way and that in front of the mirror.

Anne shook her head in wonderment. The dress had a strapless fitted bodice and a slimline long skirt with an oversized bow across the back. 'OK?' Anne seemed lost for words. 'You look stunning! Noah's eyes will be out on stalks!'

'It's not too…' Nerves attacking her all over again, Erika fingered the gown's faint cleavage.

'Don't dare change a thing,' Anne said. 'It's perfect.' She eyed Erika mistily. 'I'll bet Hillcrest has never seen a more beautiful bride…'

'Oh, Lord!' Erika gave a shaky laugh. 'My tummy feels like I've just got off a rollercoaster.' With trembling hands, she reached up to fasten the pearl choker, Noah's gift to his bride.

Kyle Matthews, looking as though he'd been given the most important job of his life, drove the bride and her father to the church in Ewen Somers' Mercedes, beribboned for the occasion.

Erika's heart was cartwheeling when her father helped her from the car. In the church porch he tucked her arm through his. 'You look lovely, darling,' he said. 'Noah is a lucky man. And a fine one,' he added, with a faintly wry smile.

Erika took a steadying breath. 'Is he here, Dad? Can you see him?'

Anne, who had arrived only seconds earlier, said briskly, 'Of course he's here!' Smiling, she executed a quick tuck and straighten of Erika's bow. Then, as the music began, she nodded encouragingly at Holly. 'Go on, baby,' she whispered. 'And don't forget to smile.'

Standing in front of the altar, Noah felt his shoulders lift in a huge steadying breath. She was here at last, his Erika, his love. She was almost to him when he turned, lifting a dark brow in admiration.

Seeing him so handsome, so dear, Erika stifled a whirlpool of nerves and found the impetus to walk the last few steps to his side.

'OK?' he murmured, reaching for her hand. Erika nodded, and clung for dear life.

'Are we ready, folks?' Standing in front of them, Tom Corelli beamed across at his two parishioners and proceeded to open his prayerbook.

Erika made her vows in a haze of happiness, hardly registering when she and Noah exchanged rings. When they were pronounced husband and wife, they kissed. And kissed again to a ripple of muted applause from the congregation.

Smiling broadly, Father Tom ushered them to an especially prepared table. And as they sat to sign the register Michael Petani sang the *Ave Maria* in a clear, sweet tenor.

'I had no idea!' Erika's whisper was shot with amazement.

'Just our little surprise for you.' Noah's expression was incredibly tender, loving. 'And I've another for you as well, Mrs Jameson.'

'Oh?' Erika blinked and blinked and tried to speak, and wondered if it were possible to overdose on sheer happiness.

Noah's smile began slowly, then widened. 'We're having a honeymoon,' he said. 'A whole week to ourselves. We've got us a locum.'

Erika's wide, beautiful mouth tucked demurely in at the edges. 'I'll be a hard act to follow,' she reminded her husband.

'Our locum's aware of that.' There was a gleam in Noah's blue eyes. 'But he put his name up anyway.'

Erika's eyes widened in disbelief. 'Are we talking about my father here?' she whispered. *'Sir?'*

Noah raised his wife's hand and casually kissed her knuckles. 'No,' he said, his lips twitching. 'We're talking about my father-in-law. *Ewen.*'

MILLS & BOON

Makes any time special

Enjoy a romantic novel from Mills & Boon®

Presents...™   *Enchanted*™   TEMPTATION®

Historical Romance™   MEDICAL ROMANCE®

MAT1

MILLS & BOON

MEDICAL ROMANCE

MOTHER TO BE by Lucy Clark

Dr Mallory Newman had always loved surgeon Nicholas Sterling but when he married her best friend, she was devastated. Now he's back, widowed and with a two year old daughter. Can his determination to win Mallory's heart survive what she has to tell him first?

DOCTORS AT ODDS by Drusilla Douglas

The last person Dr Sarah Sinclair had wanted to see on her return home was orthopaedic registrar Rory Drummond. After all, her unrequited love for him had caused her to leave in the first place. Had time changed anything or were they destined to be just friends?

A SECOND CHANCE AT LOVE by Laura MacDonald

Single mother Dr Olivia Chandler has no choice but to offer locum Dr Duncan Bradley her spare room. His resemblance to her daughter's father is unsettling but as she gets to know him, she finds herself loving him for himself. But is the feeling mutual?

Available from 7th July 2000

Available at most branches of WH Smith, Tesco, Martins, Borders, Easons, Volume One/James Thin and most good paperback bookshops

MILLS & BOON

MEDICAL ROMANCE

HEART AT RISK by Helen Shelton

Luke Geddes' appointment as Consultant Cardiologist brings him directly in contact with his ex-wife, Dr Annabel Stuart. Shocked at her change in appearance, he is dismayed to discover that what he thought was a mutual parting, was anything but for her…

GREATER THAN RICHES by Jennifer Taylor
Bachelor Doctors

Dr Alexandra Campbell is sure that Dr Stephen Spencer won't be able to cope with helping out the inner city practice. Continually at cross purposes, it's not until Stephen puts his life in danger for Alex that she finally discovers her feelings may be deeper than she thought.

MARRY ME by Meredith Webber
Book Three of a Trilogy

Dr Sarah Gilmour's new posting to Windrush Sidings brought back many memories. Seeing Tony Kemp, the love of her life, after eleven years forced her to realise how much he meant to her. Yet, for now, she needed his help as a senior police officer with an unexpected death…

Available from 7th July 2000

Available at most branches of WH Smith, Tesco, Martins, Borders, Easons, Volume One/James Thin and most good paperback bookshops

MILLS & BOON®

STRANGERS IN PARADISE

Meet Carrie, Jo, Pam and Angel...
Four women, each about to meet a
sexy stranger...
Enjoy the passion-filled nights
and long, sensual days...

Four stories in one collection

Not in My Bed!
by Kate Hoffmann

With a Stetson and a Smile
by Vicki Lewis Thompson

Wife is 4-Letter Word
by Stephanie Bond

Beguiled
by Lori Foster

Published 19th May

*Available at most branches of WH Smith, Tesco, Martins,
Borders, Easons, Volume One/James Thin
and most good paperback bookshops*

FREE

4 BOOKS
AND A SURPRISE GIFT!

We would like to take this opportunity to thank you for reading this Mills & Boon® book by offering you the chance to take FOUR more specially selected titles from the Medical Romance™ series absolutely FREE! We're also making this offer to introduce you to the benefits of the Reader Service™—

- ★ FREE home delivery
- ★ FREE monthly Newsletter
- ★ FREE gifts and competitions
- ★ Exclusive Reader Service discounts
- ★ Books available before they're in the shops

Accepting these FREE books and gift places you under no obligation to buy; you may cancel at any time, even after receiving your free shipment. Simply complete your details below and return the entire page to the address below. **You don't even need a stamp!**

YES! Please send me 4 free Medical Romance books and a surprise gift. I understand that unless you hear from me, I will receive 6 superb new titles every month for just £2.40 each, postage and packing free. I am under no obligation to purchase any books and may cancel my subscription at any time. The free books and gift will be mine to keep in any case.

MOEC

Ms/Mrs/Miss/Mr ....Initials ....
BLOCK CAPITALS PLEASE

Surname ....

Address ....

....

....Postcode ....

Send this whole page to:
UK: FREEPOST CN81, Croydon, CR9 3WZ
EIRE: PO Box 4546, Kilcock, County Kildare (stamp required)

Offer valid in UK and Eire only and not available to current Reader Service subscribers to this series. We reserve the right to refuse an application and applicants must be aged 18 years or over. Only one application per household. Terms and prices subject to change without notice. Offer expires 31st December 2000. As a result of this application, you may receive further offers from Harlequin Mills & Boon Limited and other carefully selected companies. If you would prefer not to share in this opportunity please write to The Data Manager at the address above.

Mills & Boon® is a registered trademark owned by Harlequin Mills & Boon Limited.
Medical Romance™ is being used as a trademark.

MILLS & BOON®
Makes any time special™

0006/05

By Request

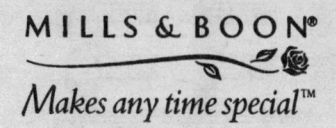

Marriages by Arrangement

A MARRIAGE HAS BEEN ARRANGED
by Anne Weale

Pierce Sutherland is the only man Holly has ever wanted, but her glamorous blonde stepsister is more his type. So when Pierce proposes a marriage of convenience, can Holly's pride allow her to accept?

TO TAME A PROUD HEART
by Cathy Williams

Francesca Wade is determined to prove her worth to her employer. Yet one night of passion has her out of Oliver Kemp's office and up the aisle—with a man too proud to love her, but too honourable to leave her!

NEVER A BRIDE by Diana Hamilton

Jake Winter was every woman's fantasy—and Claire's husband! But their marriage was a purely business arrangement—so how was Claire to tell Jake she'd fallen in love with him?

Look out for *Marriages* by Arrangement in July 2000

Available at branches of WH Smith, Tesco, Martins, Borders, Easons, Volume One/James Thin and most good paperback bookshops